Pamela was born in a small market town in Worcestershire, the eldest of seven children, in a close-knit family environment. After a rewarding career as a business manager working in Birmingham, Manchester and London, gaining an MBA, it was only on retirement that she was able to devote time to her love of writing and a second career as a clinical hypnotherapist. She considers her faith, family and friends as the most important things in her life.

Pamela Ford

IT'S ONLY ROCK & ROLL

To Eileen
Love and Best Wishes
Pamela Ford
2024

AUSTIN MACAULEY PUBLISHERS™
LONDON * CAMBRIDGE * NEW YORK * SHARJAH

Copyright © Pamela Ford 2024

The right of Pamela Ford to be identified as author of this work has been asserted by the author in accordance with sections 77 and 78 of the Copyright, Designs and Patents Act 1988.

All rights reserved. No part of this publication may be reproduced, stored in a retrieval system, or transmitted in any form or by any means, electronic, mechanical, photocopying, recording, or otherwise, without the prior permission of the publishers.

Any person who commits any unauthorised act in relation to this publication may be liable to criminal prosecution and civil claims for damages.

This is a work of fiction. Names, characters, businesses, places, events, locales, and incidents are either the products of the author's imagination or used in a fictitious manner. Any resemblance to actual persons, living or dead, or actual events is purely coincidental.

A CIP catalogue record for this title is available from the British Library.

ISBN 9781035832378 (Paperback)
ISBN 9781035832385 (ePub e-book)

www.austinmacauley.co.uk

First Published 2024
Austin Macauley Publishers Ltd®
1 Canada Square
Canary Wharf
London
E14 5AA

Chapter 1

"Do you believe in the spirit of place, Edna?" I asked. "Do you think that buildings retain the essence of what has taken place in them?"

"I really don't know, madam," she said.

I don't think she knew what I was talking about, but as always, she was far too polite to say. I sometimes wished she would say exactly what she thought instead of being the perfect employee. It sometimes would be a lot more helpful but then again, her honesty may be a little bit difficult to swallow.

I looked around me the studio looked just the same as it always had. His collection of guitars on stands lined up against the wall. Gold, silver and platinum discs, all neatly framed, were hanging on the windowless walls. They acted like an aphrodisiac the first time he brought me in here. The room was quiet and still at the moment. When the boys from the band were in here playing and writing, it was mayhem, a cacophony of sounds and rhythm. I avoided the space then which was just as well as I was very much a spare part, unwanted and overlooked until refreshments were called for.

As I leaned against the stark white wall and closed my eyes, I hoped those feelings, that joy, I had experienced all those years ago would come flooding back to me and for a moment I could feel he was holding me close to him again, his body pressed hard against me, his hands in the small of my back pulling me closer to him and his lips, his lips crushing mine with such passion.

Even now, thinking of that moment, I could feel my heart thumping in my chest and my breath coming heavy and fast. I opened my eyes and for a moment I expected to see him standing there in front of me, those piercing pale blue watery eyes looking down directly into mine. I shuddered suddenly someone must have walked over my grave, I thought.

"Are you alright, madam?" Edna asked, looking at me strangely and bringing me back to the here and now. She was a petite woman with sharp features and dark hair and eyes. She had been my rock for all the years I had known her. She had provided everything I had ever needed whilst I had been with Jack.

Like all live-in staff, she had become part of the family and got to know us as well as we knew ourselves. She was more than staff; she was as much a member of this family as any of us. I realised she most probably thought I had finally lost my mind.

"Yes, of course, I'm fine," I said, not really feeling fine at all.

"Well, I think that's all. Thank you, Edna, for everything, for all your help." I held out my hand and she took it in hers, I smiled. I think for a moment I saw a tear in her eyes. "We will all miss you terribly, madam. Where will you go?" she asked.

"Away somewhere to think about what I want for the future, somewhere I can think without any pressure from anyone," I replied.

"Please don't stay away too long," she said.

I took one last look at the place where I had been standing and took a deep breath perhaps trying to absorb the sensations I had just experienced, I handed Edna the keys that I had been holding then I quickly turned and left.

Stepping outside, Charles the chauffeur opened the door of the car. I was determined not to look back, so I strode over and entered the open door with purpose and a determination I really was not feeling.

Was I doing the right thing? Just running away like this. Shouldn't I stay and talk about the betrayal I felt? No, I needed time to clear my head, to think things through. Did I really want to live with the mistrust and heartache? I was about to start to cry again; I had to pull myself together, take a deep breath, go somewhere he couldn't pressurise me to stay, to forgive him, to start over again.

"Are we still going to the airport, madam?" Charles the chauffeur asked.

"Yes, but first can you take me to see your friend the private detective, Jason Allan? I have made an appointment, he is expecting me," I answered. "No need to rush, Charles. We have plenty of time."

I saw Charles look in the rear-view mirror at me but he made no reply.

I settled down into the plush seats of the car, all part of the trappings of being a successful rock star's wife. I was determined not to look back at the house that had been my home for the past number of years and I suddenly realised that if I decided I could no longer live with the deceit and cheating I may never see it again.

How could he do this to me? Hurt me like this? He, more than anyone, knew what Ben's cheating had done to me. The hurt never really goes away, you hide it, bury it away but it stays under the surface as you move on, but when it happens again, the hurt resurfaces and seems to increase because you remember the time before and it just multiplies the feeling.

I looked ahead and saw the driveway stretching in front of us. Don't look back, no regrets, I whispered to myself. I was so determined to look to the future, take some time to sort my head out and get back to some semblance of order in my life. Then that song came on the radio, that one song that was playing all those years ago when it all began. I realised that the fates were against me and as I listened, the years slipped away and I was back to the start of everything.

Chapter 2

"Did he just grab you?" my friend Jane asked, looking back at the two boys who were now standing a little behind us.

"Mm, yes," I answered.

"I think I'll go tell him to shove off," she continued rather aggressively. "Who is he anyway?"

"I think his name is Jack. I don't really know him but I think he went to the same school as Ben."

Ben was a boy I had been seeing for a little while. He was tall and fair, terribly handsome and our families were friends. He was training to be a doctor and had started his internship at the local hospital.

"His friend is a bit of alright," she said, looking directly at the boy Jack was now speaking to.

"You're supposed to be engaged," I reminded her.

"That's OK; you're allowed to look as long as you don't touch," but I knew her very well and if she had the opportunity she would be touching, engaged or not.

"What did this Jack want, anyway?" she asked, still eyeing the friend of Jacks.

"He told me he loved me," I replied.

"Oh, come on, you have to be joking. A perfect stranger you don't know just comes up to you and tells you he loves you, since when?" Jane laughed.

"I don't know that's all he said."

And it was, he had just grabbed my arm and said, "Do you realise just how much I love you?"

I was quite taken aback, speechless. He must have thought I was a nincompoop not to have replied. I had just looked at him and continued walking by.

The evening continued just like the other evenings we had spent in this nightclub. It was a regular haunt of ours and as Jane had Tuesday evenings off from her fiancé, this is where we chose to come. We knew most of the regulars and they always had a live group so it was lively and a good evening.

Jane was one of my best friends and we had known each other since we were small children. Our families had lived quite close to each other and as we were the same age, we had been friends all our lives. She was a very attractive girl with unusual looks, large dark eyes that filled her face. Boys found her attractive and she was always popular, although a terrible flirt. She was engaged to a young man called Cameron whom she met whilst we were out together one night a little while ago.

I hadn't realised until then that the events we had been going to over the previous few weeks had been to casually run into him, eventually it seemed to work because he had noticed us and started up a conversation.

However, it nearly all went terribly wrong as it seemed to be me he wanted to get to know, but Jane was not going to let that happen and she very quickly pushed herself between us and made sure she was the one he was concentrating on. I could see the attraction.

Cameron was slightly older than us and was obviously well off. He drove a sports car, was expensively well-dressed and did not mind spending his money extravagantly. After a very short time, Jane very quickly became engaged to Cameron and as an engagement present, he paid for her to have driving lessons and when she passed her driving test, he bought her a car a beautiful dark blue mini which enabled us to go further afield on her nights off.

This gave her a lot of freedom and an endless opportunity to meet other boys. I somehow always seemed to be embroiled in these encounters, she seemed to use me as her cover. I always thought that Cameron knew what she was up to but he turned a blind eye and just went on indulging her. It's strange how people ignore things they can't face up to or deal with head-on.

We became separated during the evening, but I was talking and dancing with other people and I knew she would resurface at some time. She would be flirting with someone or another, making them feel they were the only boy in the world. It made me very uncomfortable as I knew Cameron, her fiancé, very well and I had to be careful what I said when we met in case I let something slip that I shouldn't.

"Can I buy you a drink?" It was Jack.

"Yes, OK," I replied. I was a bit nervous remembering what he had said to me earlier.

We sat in one of the small alcoves of the dimly lit bar and it gave me time to study him. He was tall and very slim. His hairstyle made him look a little like Steve Marriot from the Small Faces, a popular group at the time. He had beautiful pale blue eyes that, when you looked into them, made you imagine you were looking into the blue of the ocean with sunlight sparkling on the surface. I could see now that he was quite handsome and I wondered why I had never really noticed him before.

"I bet I shocked you earlier by saying what I did?" he said.

"I was quite surprised. You certainly caught my attention," I replied, smiling.

"It's the truth. I think from the first moment I saw you with Ben, I have been thinking of you," he said, making me blush. I found it difficult to understand that I had never even noticed him and here I was, the object of his attention.

"I don't know what to say except I'm terribly flattered or do you say that to every girl you meet?" I asked.

"No, definitely not. You're the first and only one," he said, looking straight into my eyes.

"Look, I have a boyfriend already," I said. "It would be wrong of me to start up a relationship with someone else. It doesn't seem right even having this conversation with you."

"Yes, I know," he said. "Where's Ben tonight?" he suddenly asked.

"He's busy working and studying we don't spend much time together," I replied.

"Is it serious between the two of you?" he asked.

"I'm not sure," I replied, a little taken aback. "It's early days. We're good together and seem to get on OK. Do you know him very well?" I asked.

"We were at school together in fact he was our head boy and we are good friends, I wouldn't like to upset him in any way. He was always a swot; he'll get on very well, as he's always been very focussed."

"Yes, he is," I answered, not knowing what I was meant to say. "What do you do?"

Jack gave a little laugh in the back of his throat. "Nothing as grand as studying to be a doctor," he said. "I am currently stacking shelves in a supermarket but I want to play in a band, music is all I can think about sometimes, Fact is I have an audition next week, well my older brother has an audition and I am tagging along to see if I can get in on the act."

"How well do you think you will do?" I asked.

"Well, I'm keen and I play the guitar every free minute I have, but at the end of the day, it's if you fit in with the other members of the group. I am just keeping my fingers crossed."

"I hope you do well. If it's what you really want."

"Thanks," he said, looking straight at me. "It's not all I want, though."

I wasn't quite sure what to say. Was he implying he wanted me to be part of his future? "Will you let me know how you get on? I would like to know."

He took my hand and nodded his head. He was just about to say something else when I heard Jane's voice.

"Come on, you lovebirds. It's time we were going." She had her arm around the neck of Jack's friend and they looked as if they had been very much together. So much for not touching, I thought.

Jane kissed Jack's friend goodbye and before I had the opportunity to say anything to Jack, she had pulled me away and we were on our way out. Jane never gave anyone else the slightest thought when she was ready to leave, that's when we left. We soon sat in her car, the one that her finance, Cameron, had bought her and on our way home.

I suddenly felt I had a lot to think about. Jack had put thoughts into my head. Was my relationship with Ben serious? I know Mom liked the idea that my boyfriend was a potential doctor. I had not thought that far ahead before, but now I needed to think more about how I felt about him and whether was he what I wanted, I suddenly felt as if I had just been coasting lacking any real direction.

I was being led by what other people wanted of me. My mother wanted me married to Ben, a doctor, which was her objective not necessarily mine. My best friend was using me to enable her to satisfy her needs and Ben wanted a girlfriend that looked good on his arm and would fit into the lifestyle he had planned out for himself.

I had let this happen, just going along with what everyone else wanted of me and I now realised it wasn't enough anymore. I wanted to be in charge of my future, whatever that was to be. What did I want of myself?

Chapter 3

It was a few weeks later when I saw Jack again. Ben and I were in the local pub, which happened to be next to the hospital where Ben was currently working. He lived in the hospital accommodation so it was convenient to meet here.

We were quietly sitting in one of the many alcoves, not saying very much when Jack and a pretty little blonde girl came in. Ben called them over and the blonde sat down next to me.

"I'm starving; can you get me some crisps?" she asked Jack.

"Hello," he said to us both. "You don't mind if we join you? It's quite busy in here tonight, isn't it?"

"No, of course not," said Ben. "How are you? I haven't seen you for a while. What have you been doing?"

Telling your girlfriend he loves her, I thought quietly to myself.

"I'll be back in a minute, we can catch up. Can I get anyone a drink?"

"No, we're fine, thanks," said Ben.

Jack went to the bar.

"Hello," said Ben to the blonde sat next to me. "I'm Ben and this is my girlfriend."

"Yes, I know," she interrupted before Ben could mention my name. "Jack's told me about you. You're studying to be a doctor, aren't you? I'm Marie, Jack's girlfriend." She held out her hand to Ben, ignoring me altogether.

"Nice to meet you," he said.

Jack come back and sat next to Marie. She immediately flung her arms around his neck and said, "Oh I have missed you," and kissed him on the cheek.

He looked slightly embarrassed but smiled and kissed her back.

Ben and Jack started to talk to each other, catching up on friends and things that had been happening. I had time to look at Marie, who was still clinging to Jack's neck. She was small and slightly chubby but very pretty. Her hair, which looked naturally blonde, fell in curls around her face. She wore very little makeup, but then she didn't seem to need it. She was bubbly and happy and I could see how attractive she would appear to any boy. Jack's deep and abiding love for me seemed to be faltering somewhat.

"Well, they said they liked me and I start rehearsing with them next week. They call themselves The Testators." I suddenly heard Jack saying. "I couldn't believe my luck. I only went to support Stephen but they asked if I played and when I said yes, they asked me to audition. They have lost their lead singer and they asked me to sing something for them, so I did and they said OK, when could I join them? Can you believe it?"

"Well done," said Ben. "Don't forget your friends when you become famous."

"Well, I think that may be a long time off, but at least it's a start."

Ben stood up. "I think this calls for another drink. What are we having?"

"I'll have another pint," said Marie. "I'll have to pay a visit to the little girl's room first, though." She stood up, finally letting go of Jack's neck.

Both Ben and Marie left, giving me the opportunity to speak to Jack.

"I'm glad you were successful with the audition," I said to Jack. "Did Stephen do OK as well?"

"No," said Jack. "I think he was a little bit old for them. His style of playing is different from mine; I don't think he was what they were looking for. He was a bit disappointed."

"That's a shame but I am pleased for you if it's what you want."

"It's part of what I want," he said, looking directly at me. "I can't stop thinking about you. I need to speak to you. Can we meet?"

I looked over at Ben at the bar he had his back to us and strangely I felt guilty.

"When?" I asked.

"Tomorrow, at the Rose and Crown, about 8 o'clock," he said.

I saw Ben returning from the bar with our drinks.

"Yes, OK," I said quickly.

The rest of the evening passed pleasantly enough. Although I was thinking about Jack all the time, it was difficult to follow the conversation.

Whilst Ben was driving me home, he asked what I thought of Marie. I said she seemed pleasant I liked her.

"You'll never guess what Jack told me about her," he said. "He says she's a sex maniac, that she will have her hands in his pants before they get to the car."

He laughed, thinking it was funny but it was an image I could have done without having in my mind.

The following day seemed to drag on forever. I took extra care getting ready that night and when I looked in the mirror, I was pleased with the result. I arrived deliberately late; I didn't want to be the first there. Jack was standing at the bar looking towards the door as I walked in. As I approached him, he took my hand and kissed me on the cheek in the most natural manner.

"You look stunning," he said. "Shall we sit over there?" He already had my drink. I thought he must have been certain I would turn up. We walked over to a table at the back of the room.

I felt nervous and guilty; suddenly feeling the situation was unreal.

"I don't think I should be here," I said.

"I know, I feel guilty too," said Jack. "But we haven't done anything to feel guilty about. I have to speak to you before I can move on. I can't stop thinking about you. You're in my head."

"I don't understand you hardly know me. We have never even had a proper conversation," I replied.

"I know. I have asked myself why I feel this way. I just do. You're the first thing I think about in the morning and the last thing at night before I fall asleep."

"It's just an obsession," I said. "Marie seems lovely. You will move on."

"I need to know if I have any chance of being with you. Do you love Ben? If you do, I will accept it and that will be the end. I will never contact you again."

"I don't know. I like Ben. He's nice to me, we get on. Our parents are friends. Is he the love of my life? I don't know. You're pressurising me to speak of feelings I have not thought about. Do I have feelings for you? I don't know you. What do you want me to say?"

"I want you to say you feel the same way about me, but I can tell that's not going to happen. Is It?"

"Look, Ben was talking about marriage last night. I had to say the same thing to him as I am saying to you now. I'm not sure it's what I want. In fact, I'm beginning to feel I don't know what I want anymore. It feels too soon to be making plans for the rest of my life," I explained. "I guess if I felt I loved him, I wouldn't be here with you now."

"What did he say?" Jack asked.

"He said he understood. He knew what he wanted but he was willing to wait. There was no hurry."

"I don't think I can do the same. Thinking about you with someone else is purgatory."

"I'm sorry," I said and I did genuinely mean it. I reached for his hand. He clasped mine and brought it to his lips, kissing my fingers so gently. My heart skipped a beat. It was extremely flattering to have someone like Jack feeling this way about me, but it felt like a betrayal of my relationship with Ben. I could not respond to Jack the way perhaps I would like to. If I really reciprocated Jack's feelings, I should speak to Ben first and be honest with him about the way I felt.

Jack must have realised my reluctance to say anything. He looked directly into my eyes and smiled an understanding sort of smile and I hoped he understood the way I was feeling.

"I think we should leave," he said.

He walked me to my car. The weather changed. It was cold and whilst we had been inside, there had been a covering of snow on the ground. There were flakes swirling around us and I felt cold. I opened the car door and turned around to reluctantly say goodbye to Jack.

"Before I go, I want you to have this," he said, putting a small silver cross and chain into my hand.

"I couldn't possibly take it," I replied, trying to give it back to him.

"No," he said. "I want you to have it. It was my mother's. She told me to give it to the girl I fell in love with. So it belongs to you."

Before I could say anything else, he took me in his arms and kissed me a long, hard, sweet goodbye kiss and was gone.

I sat in the car for a few moments, trying to gather my thoughts, feeling something was lost and I wasn't sure what. As I reversed out of the space, I noticed our footprints in the snow. Two walking together and one walking away into the night. The image remained in my mind for a long time and I felt sad and wondered if the feeling I now had would last longer than the footprints in the snow.

Chapter 4

My mother believed that being the wife of a doctor was all any girl could wish for or want from life, it brought a certain status but after the conversation with Jack I started to think long and hard about my future again and what I wanted. I felt that just being a wife and mother was not enough for me, even if it was for my mother.

I had a good job in administration at the hospital but I could not see much of a future in this. I wanted more. The discussion with my parents that followed these revelations was torturous.

"University? A degree? Whatever for?" Mother asked and my father, I felt, reluctantly went along with her. My mother suggested a college course she had seen advertised and for a moment I listened interested in what she was saying. But it turned out to be a Cordon Bleu cookery course. She said it would be useful when entertaining Ben's business colleagues. So, if my parents were not willing to support me, I would have to do it the hard way and on my own.

I continued to work full time and studied for a degree in psychology in my spare time evenings and weekends. It was hard but I managed it. Ben and I went on seeing each other but with both of us studying so hard, we spent very little time together.

I eventually obtained a good degree that enabled me to go on and study for a master's in psychology. Eventually, six years after starting, I became a clinical psychologist and was lucky enough to find a job in the hospital where Ben was now a junior doctor. He had decided to specialise in paediatrics and was building a good reputation.

Eventually, I said yes to one of his many proposals of marriage and Mommy and Daddy gave us a big white wedding. It seemed that my mother's dreams had come true. A Daughter married to a doctor, she could hardly contain herself.

The wedding itself was every girl's dream. My dress cost a fortune and was covered in tiny pearls with a long heavy lace train. When I came down the stairs at home to where dad was waiting for me, he started to cry.

"Hey, what's this?" I asked. "It should be a happy day."

"I've never seen anyone look so beautiful," he said. "I am so proud of you and everything you have achieved; I should have been more supportive of you and ignored your mother. I am so sorry."

"Don't be, I couldn't have asked for better parents," I said to him, putting my arm around him and kissing him on the cheek. "You made me stand on my own two feet. It was good for me. I am not beholden to anyone. Now let's get this show on the road. Are you ready?"

"Yes, I hope Ben realises what a lucky man he is."

"I'm sure he does."

The wedding was in a small village church close to our family home and was decked out with all white flowers. My two little bridesmaids were nieces of Bens and behaved so beautifully all day. The church was tiny so we were only able to invite family and close friends to the service itself, but the reception was at a local hotel and over 100 people attended this with the festivities carrying on until the early hours of the morning.

As with all brides, I was totally exhausted afterwards. The run-up to the wedding and organising everything, then the day itself, you operate on sheer adrenaline but when it's over, it's like hitting a brick wall.

We honeymooned in Jamaica, a present from Ben's parents, which was wonderful. It was the first time Ben and I had ever really spent a long time alone together solely in each other's company and it seemed strange at first but we knew each so well as we had been together for a long time and it seemed right. We settled into married life very happily.

The memory of Jack and those footprints in the snow had almost disappeared.

From time to time, we came across articles about Jack and his rock band. Some were about their success, others about wrecked hotel rooms, trouble with girls, drinking and drugs, the general lifestyle of a rock group. One member of the band had died from an overdose very early in their careers. It seemed a different world to the one I knew.

Life was good for Ben and me. We moved into a modern flat close to the city centre and both our careers took off. Ben became a paediatric surgeon and I eventually went into private practice with a friend I had studied with at university called Amos.

I always thought that the name Amos conjures up an image of an old man with grey whiskery sideburns wearing a flat cap and racing whippets but Amos was the complete opposite. He was tall with dark hair and intense dark eyes, always immaculately dressed in the way only gay men seem to achieve. The profession we had chosen was still very much heterosexually male dominated, so that made us both outsiders to a degree.

We got on well together and were good friends. He was like my career husband. I sometimes seemed to spend more time with Amos than I did with Ben we almost finished each other's sentences we knew each other so well. Our minds were always on the same wavelength, we rarely disagreed and our business was very successful because we both wanted the same things from it.

This relationship worked and we remained friends all our lives. We had the same mindset and values; we were a couple in every sense except sexually. We both agreed right from the beginning of our partnership to be always open and honest with each other and we always were. Sometimes too brutally honest but it worked.

Three years after the start of our partnership we opened our first clinic together dealing mostly with addictive personalities. Dad helped me raise the money (without Mom knowing) and Amos had some wealthy gay friends that were also willing to invest. The clinic was so successful we were able to repay the investments after the second year and open another clinic.

The second clinic had large premises in north London and was never empty. There was always more demand than appointments available. We also hired rooms on Harley Street and had clients from all walks of life; even a minor royal at one stage.

Whilst our careers took off, Ben and I lived well. We had plenty of friends and were financially quite well off. We had holidays abroad and eventually moved into a lovely house in the city suburbs. We discussed having a family, there was continuous pressure from Mom about grandchildren (or the lack of them), but Ben enjoyed our lifestyle and there always seemed plenty of time to plan for the future.

We were both busy, successful people and our marriage worked or so I thought. Ben always said he was proud of me and what I had achieved. As busy as we both were, we realised how important it was to set aside time to be with each other. One of the ways this worked was to book time away from our work and get away together on holiday.

Although on a recent holiday to the Maldives, Ben had seemed distant and distracted but I put it down to the recent loss of one of his young patients. The holiday was relaxing.

The Maldives were a beautiful group of Islands in the Indian Ocean. Each island held one hotel. Our room was actually on stilts out on the water. We swam, snorkelled, sunbathed on the beach, made love under the stars. It was an ideal holiday but Ben still never spoke about what was troubling him and when we returned home, he was back to being the same as he was before we went away.

I talked to him about it but he said it was nothing; he was just tired and overworked and that the holiday would sort it out but it didn't. He seemed more distant than ever after we came home and I eventually asked Amos if he had noticed a difference in him.

"I have noticed that he seems a bit distracted," said Amos. "But he does work long hours and he has taken on a lot more responsibility lately now he is head of department."

"Yes, I know, but work has never been a problem before; in fact, he thrives on it. I hope he's not ill and doesn't feel as if he can share with me any problems, we've always been able to talk to each other in the past about any worries either of us might have."

"Well, you can only support him until he's ready to tell you what's wrong," Amos said, putting his arm around me. I think he could tell that I was concerned.

"I know. Perhaps I'm just being over-sensitive. I'll just have to be patient and wait till he's ready to share with me whatever is up with him."

Amos and I eventually opened our third clinic. We decided to celebrate the opening with a party, inviting all our staff from the other clinics as a thank you for their commitment and hard work. It was held in the large, airy reception area of the new clinic. This clinic had been purposely built for a purpose rather than a converted old building. We employed a catering company and I felt we had finally achieved the success Amos and I had been working so hard for. They say pride comes before a fall, don't they?

At the gathering, which was in full swing, with everyone enjoying the free bar, a young woman came up to me and asked to speak to me privately. This very often happened with people at the most inopportune moments and I asked if it could wait until the following day as I needed to attend to my many guests. But seeing her distress, I reluctantly agreed and took her into one of the side rooms and asked how I could help.

"I'm having Ben's baby," she said suddenly.

I thought I had heard her incorrectly or perhaps she was speaking about a Ben I did not know and was quite taken aback.

"I'm sorry," I said. "What did you say?"

"He loves me and we're having a baby."

I felt as if I had been punched in the chest. I could not catch my breath. I looked closer at this girl. She was small with dark hair and eyes and I realised I had seen her somewhere before but could not quite place where. She stood there with a smirk on her face, seemingly enjoying my distress.

"I don't believe you," I said shakingly. "Ben would never hurt me like that."

"Really?" the girl said. "Perhaps you don't know him as well as you think you do."

At that point, Ben walked in on us. He looked horrified when he saw who was with me. I looked at him and asked, "Is this true?"

"Go on, tell her, you promised you would," said the young woman.

"I'm so sorry," Ben said, looking more and more distressed. "I did not want you to find out this way."

"Oh and what way would you have liked me to find out?" I asked. "Over a candlelight dinner for two or perhaps after we had made love one evening, casually saying, oh by the way, there's a little scrubber that happens to be having my baby."

By now, my voice was raised and I was losing control. I started to shake with fury and my distress was incalculable.

"Ben, are you going to allow her to speak about me that way?" said the little scrubber.

"Please, can't we talk about this calmer, somewhere else?" Ben asked, taking hold of my arm. I shrugged his hold off me and picked up an item off the desk and threw it at the wall beside his head. At that moment Amos came in and closed the door behind him.

"What on earth is going on?" he asked. "You can be heard outside."

"Why don't you ask this bastard and the little scrubber over there?" I said.

I turned around and left the room. I could not trust myself to stay. I was shaking so much I left the party and got into the first taxi I saw. I gave our home address and bust in tears, hardly being able to catch my breath.

What I was going to do when I got there? I had no idea. It can't possibly be true. Ben would not do this to me. So this was what the last few weeks had been about. Here was me being so concerned for Ben, fearing that perhaps he was ill and had been unable to tell me and all this time he had been having an affair with another woman. I was sobbing so hard even the taxi driver began to look distressed.

When I got in doors, I paced the sitting room up and down. Everything I saw took on a memory of Ben and my life together. The coffee table was a 1st-year anniversary present from Ben's parents, the rug we had bought together in Morocco and it had been such a laugh trying to get it home.

Why had he done this? We had everything a couple could wish for. If Ben had wanted children, I was quite happy to start a family; in fact, it was Ben that seemed reluctant. The physical pain I felt was unbearable, my chest tightened and I began to wonder if I was going to have a heart attack.

By the time Ben arrived, I was a little calmer; I had stopped sobbing uncontrollably but was still terribly distressed.

"I'm so sorry," he said. "I would not have hurt you for the world."

I then burst into tears again, shaking so much I could not speak.

"Please don't cry," Ben said, putting his arm around me. "I can't bear it."

"Why?" I managed to ask.

"Please don't think I've been cheating on you having an affair or anything like that. She's a nurse I work with," he said. "I get used to them throwing themselves at me. They all want to snare a doctor. It was just a one-night stand."

"Well, that makes it OK then," I said.

"No, of course, it doesn't. I was tired. It had been a particularly bad day and after a few drinks in the hospital bar, I relaxed and drinking on an empty stomach affected me more than it should have done. You know I'm not a big drinker. It just happened. I regretted it immediately. When she told me she was pregnant, I could not believe it."

"Oh, really," I said. "You are a doctor, surely you know how these things happen." My sarcasm knew no bounds.

I saw Ben wince.

"I have told her I will take responsibility for the baby and provide for them but I don't want my marriage to end," he said. "I still love you, I always will please, please forgive me."

"I don't know if I can, Ben," I said. "I need time to think. Time to think things through. I am hurting so much, my head's all over the place."

"I understand, please believe me that I can't bear the thought that I have hurt you. Please, please forgive me. I know we can get through this. We're strong as a couple. I have never loved anyone else, losing you will be unbearable. I'll give you some space and time if that's what you need. I'll pack an overnight case and stay at the hospital for a few nights. Let me know when you're ready to talk."

"What's her name?" I asked him quietly.

"Jessica," he said. "Jess. Why do you want to know?"

"I need a name to hate," I said.

At that, he left the room. I heard him upstairs and eventually, heard him leave. The house was silent. I sat down and just cried. I could not stop. I must have fallen to sleep totally exhausted. When I woke, the house was in darkness. I went upstairs to bed, undressed and fell instantly asleep. The next morning, I was woken by the doorbell and banging on the front door. It was Amos.

"Are you OK?" he asked. "I was so worried about you."

"No, I am not OK," I answered. "In fact, I feel numb. I have no idea how to feel. It's just so unreal."

"Let's make a cup of coffee and sit and talk," he said, taking off his coat and heading for the kitchen.

That's what we did. He made me breakfast and I eat. I did not realise just how hungry I was. We talked for hours and afterwards, Amos said he would help in any way he could, I just had to ask. He said I should not decide on anything straight away but think it through and decide what I wanted. Go away from the pressure of anyone trying to make me decide on any course of action. It needed to be my decision. He offered to look after the practice so I could take as much time as I needed and then he left me to decide what I was going to do.

By the next morning, I was packed and on my way to a friend who lived in northern Italy near Verona. She was always asking me to stay so I took her up on her offer. Jenny and I had been at school together and we remained good friends. She was married to an Italian and they owned vineyards in northern Italy.

I needed to be somewhere else so I could think without any interference or pressure from any other person. Amos was the only one who knew my whereabouts. I just told Ben I was going away and would be in touch when I was ready. I felt he did not deserve any more explanation than that.

Chapter 5

Italy healed me. I arrived a total wreck but left refreshed and whole again, back in control of my thoughts and my life and certain of what I wanted.

In the beginning, my friend Jenny fussed over me like a mother hen. Nothing was too much trouble. She sat and listened to me for hours, never disagreeing with me or telling me what to do. She just listened. She held me close when I sobbed and believe me, I sobbed. I felt I had never been so unhappy.

Eventually, the sunshine, wine and friendship cleared my mind and I started thinking about my future and, of course, there was also Roberto.

Roberto was Jenny's brother-in-law, the youngest of her husband's brothers. He was young, fit with those dark sultry Italian looks. The vineyard was very much a family business and each member of the family seemed to have a part to play in the running of the business. On a Sunday, it was a time to rest, go to church and celebrate the week's success. There were grandparents, parents and children all together for lunch, a siesta in the afternoon and chat, more food and lots of local wine in the evening. The days were magical.

After a short while, when my head had started to clear, I started to think about how the end of a relationship is like a bereavement. The loss, pain, unhappiness, the inevitability of the despair and emptiness it brought and how to understand how anyone could recover.

I had already started to write a self-help book, mostly for myself and having the time now, I completed the task. It helped me to focus on therapies I had previously learnt and refreshed a lot of the basic help and mind exercises that could be useful to anyone in the same position as I found myself. I contacted Amos and asked for more time away. He was fine with this. He was coping everything was going well.

The one conclusion I did reach, however, was I knew my marriage to Ben was over. If I could forgive him, there would always be a child between him and Jessica. I could not forgive Ben's betrayal and I decided I needed to tell him I wanted a divorce. I did not want to do this by a telephone call, but I was not ready to come home yet. It was a torturous conversation with Ben but I built up enough courage and went ahead. I contacted a solicitor to act on my behalf and asked Ben to only contact me through him.

The pain was still raw; every time I thought about him being a father, I felt it should have been me pregnant and looking forward to the birth of our first child. I hoped we could settle everything amicably and eventually after a lot of pleading from Ben I think he understood my feelings and knew there was no going back for me. Although he begged me to reconsider, he said he still loved me and had never loved anyone else. He wanted forgiveness but I couldn't, I hurt too much.

Roberto became my lover and bonked me senseless until no other thought remained in my head. Believe or believe it or not, I had only ever had sex with Ben. I did not feel guilty about Roberto or regret anything about our relationship. He was just what I needed.

In fact, I have come to the conclusion that every woman at least once in their life should have an Italian lover. I, of course, did not include this as one of the therapies in my book. Well, even Marilyn Monroe had Joe DiMaggio. Roberto was part of my therapy and it worked. We did not have long discussions about life or love; in fact, that would have been very difficult as neither of us spoke the same language. But we laughed, made endless love and for a short time we realised it was what we both needed.

Altogether I was in Italy for five months and when it was time to leave, I felt whole again and ready to face the world. It was hard saying goodbye to Roberto but we both realised it was a love affair, not a lifelong relationship. We both took away the knowledge that we had shared something good between us.

It was in Italy I discovered my love of opera. Jenny was always an opera fan and she took me several times to the open-air theatre in Verona. These nights were magical. Sitting under the stars in the warmth of the evening listening to Madam Butterfly, Aida and what was to become my favourite Turandot. At first, I went to indulge Jenny but after a very short time, I was hooked and could not keep away. It's a love I have never lost and am so grateful to Jenny for teaching me how music can lift the soul.

According to my solicitor, Ben agreed to a quick divorce. I thought perhaps he wanted to be married before the birth but in the end, Ben never married Jess, the mother of his children.

In my divorce settlement, Ben kept the family house, after all, he was the one that was going to have a family, but the settlement was generous enough for me to buy a country cottage in a small Worcestershire village I had always liked. I also kept the property in the Algarve we had bought between us celebrating our 5th wedding anniversary and eventually there was enough money from my book sales (yes, even without the Roberto therapy being mentioned). It sold very well, enough to put a large deposit on a modern new London flat in Chelsea Harbour where I stayed during the week when I was working.

The publishing company wanted a series of self-help books and gave me a very generous amount of money to tie me to them. Life again seemed promising and Amos and I continued with our successful practice we even opened our first clinic in Arizona in America where there was a lot of need.

Amos had friends and family there and the desert, heat and isolation, seemed to be ideal for a retreat and a holistic clinic. Our clinics were never empty, there was always a waiting list and we took a decision to take a percentage of non-paying NHS patients to compensate for some of the success we were experiencing. In a small way, it helped Amos and I think we were giving something back to society.

Ben's little nurse Jess gave birth to twin boys and when I heard, I cried all that day. It hurt, I felt they should have been my twin boys, but of course, they weren't and I compensated by booking a holiday with a girlfriend to New York. We shopped, we went to the Met and we laughed and thoroughly enjoyed ourselves. Did it still hurt? Yes, of course, it did more than I could ever explain.

Chapter 6

Jack and his group achieved a great deal of success in America but success in the UK and the rest of the world soon followed. They appeared on television and in newspapers and magazines. I was always curious to read about him. His career took off as a solo singer and the group became more of a backing group, with Jack taking the lead. I knew he had married Marie and they had two children, a boy named William and a girl named Christine.

After several years, there was a highly publicised divorce. It was very acrimonious and every detail of the mudslinging was reported with relish by the press. Stories of the millions in a settlement that Marie received changed in each article that I read. But it would be many years from the time of our last meeting before we met again.

My self-help books became very successful and eventually, I completed a series of six. They sold very well all over the world and during the following years I completed book signing tours in several countries.

It was when I was in Vancouver in Canada and had been there completing the last three days of a gruelling schedule of a Canadian book signing tour that our paths crossed again. Although I loved Canada, the space, the air, the outlook of its people and the real effort they made towards conservation, I felt I was ready for home.

There had been some lovely experiences during the 28 days I had spent here. Whilst driving down one of the highways during the tour, the chauffeur had pulled over and said, "Look there."

Quite close by the edge of the road in the trees sat a mother bear and two cubs, oblivious to the world passing by. I was enthralled. Even in the small towns we passed through, we saw elk just grazing by the side of the road.

However, after 28 days of signing my books and chatting to so many people, all of whom had a problem or a trouble to recount, I felt worn out. They all liked my books and said how much they had helped and of course I was pleased but I just wanted to be home.

There had also been talks with a Canadian Health Group about opening clinics in Canada. I thought success brings great rewards but also lots of work. I loved my work but I was suddenly feeling jaded. As soon as I got home, I was booking a holiday, an island somewhere where I could just relax and unwind, the Maldives again perhaps.

"We will pick you up about 6 o'clock and take you to the airport if that's OK with you?" said Celia when we got back to the hotel. She was the publisher's representative here in Canada and had been with me the whole time I had been here. She was a young, energetic, pretty girl who had organised the whole tour with such efficiency for the past 26 days I really admired her skills and thought I could do with someone like you in my life at home.

In fact, the business could do with someone like her. I thought I must speak to Amos about a PA. I am sure we could afford it after all the business was a runaway success. We were both working harder than ever and we had increased the number of partners we had but we still continued working and expanding. There never seemed to be enough time to relax and enjoy the success we were achieving.

"Yes, that's fine," I answered Celia. I thought that would give me some time to pack, have a shower and rest for a couple of hours before being on my way.

The hotel was in absolute chaos; evidently, a rock group was staying there and fans had besieged every aspect of the premises trying to get in. We had quite a job proving we were actual residents before being allowed in. I suddenly thought of Jack and wondered if this was the sort of thing that happened to him.

Celia came with me to the desk and then left, saying she would see me later. I made my way to the lift feeling exhausted. However, when getting to my room, I completed my packing, showered and set the alarm for 5 o'clock, then lay on the bed. I must have fallen straight to sleep because the next thing I realised was that the alarm was ringing.

I felt better, quite refreshed and I quickly finished getting dressed, putting on my makeup and collecting all my belongings. I made a quick check of the drawers and cupboards in the suite, making sure nothing had been left behind when there was a knock on the door.

It was Celia. "Are you ready? The cars waiting," she said when I opened the door.

"Yes," I said. "Just checking that I have everything."

"OK, let's go then, shall we?" she said. "I had a terrible job actually getting into the hotel again. There's security everywhere stopping the fans of this group. Some had managed to get into the lobby somehow," she said, grabbing the handle of my case and leaving the room, heading for the lift.

"I wish we had time to hang around a bit and meet them. It's a shame we're leaving, never mind." She always chattered away like this.

I didn't feel the same; I just wanted to be home.

The lift arrived and we got in. Celia pressed the button for the lobby and the lift moved off, only to stop at the next floor down and a group of four or five men got in. The lift was not spacious and suddenly felt very cramped.

I felt a dig in my ribs. It was Celia's elbow. "It's them," she hissed under her breath.

I looked up and there he was, right in front of me. I thought he looked exactly the same as I remembered him. He was so close I could feel his breath on my forehead and the smell of the scent of the soap he had used to wash.

So many years since the last time I had stood this close to him and I thought he looks just the same. His hair was blonder now and quite long, the epitome of a rock star. He had in his hands one of those small handheld gaming machines that was all the rage at the moment and he didn't look up straight away. He turned it off then and put it in his pocket and looked directly at me.

He won't recognise me, I thought, not after all these years and he didn't at first. Then a look crossed his face, he smiled. I smiled shyly back and I could tell he did recognise me.

"I can't believe it," he said. "Is it really you? You look exactly the same. What are you doing here?"

Suddenly all eyes were on us, everyone in the lift was looking at us both including Celia whose jaw had dropped to the floor and she was stood there with her mouth wide open.

"Hello," I said quite inadequately.

Jack noticed my case beside me. "You're not leaving, are you?" he asked.

"Yes, I'm on my way to the airport," I replied.

"No, you can't be," he said, grabbing my hand. "It's been so long. Can't you delay your departure and give us some time to get reacquainted?"

The lift arrived in the lobby and the doors opened; although no one got out, they were all listening to our conversation.

I looked at Celia. "Do we have ten minutes?" I asked her.

She was still looking stunned but came to her senses quickly.

"Yes, of course. I'll go tell the driver."

As we all moved out of the lift Jack said, "Can you give me a few minutes lads?" to the bemused guys that had entered the lift with him.

He pulled me to one side of the lobby and I noticed he was still holding my hand.

"Is there no way you can put off your journey for a few days?" he asked. "It would be good to catch up; I can't believe you're here."

"I'm sorry, I'm expected back home, I've been here nearly a month," I said, suddenly wishing I could say something else.

"There's no husband or anyone special waiting for you back home, is there?" he asked. There was a look of dismay on his face.

"No, there's no husband," I said and I saw him smile.

"I'm going to be touring until Christmas; I don't get back until 6th December," he said, sounding disappointed. "Where are you living? Are you still local?"

"I have a cottage in South Worcestershire but I spend a lot of time in London for work," I replied. "What about you? Where do you live?"

"I'm in the Cotswolds, so that's not too far from you."

I could see Celia coming back into the lobby. She stopped and started talking to the other members of the group as they stood between the door and Jack and me.

"Put your number on my phone," he said, handing me his phone. I took it and dialled my number, which started ringing right away.

"Now we have each other's number, can I call you?" he asked.

"Yes, of course," I said. "I have to go. I'm sorry."

"Yes, so am I," he said.

"Bye," I said and turned and left.

"I can't believe you know Jack London," Celia said, opening the door of the limo. "He's my absolute favourite, I'm his biggest fan."

"I knew him years ago. We have not met for 'bout many years."

"Judging by the way he looked on seeing you, I don't think it will be long before you see him again."

"We will have to see," I replied, hoping it would be very soon.

"So that's the one, is it?" asked Keith, the bass guitarist, to Jack later as they were in their tour bus travelling towards that night's venue.

"Sorry, what did you say?" replied Jack rather distractedly.

"She's the one, I can tell. You've always said there was one that meant everything but got away. I can tell that was her just by the way you looked at her. I guess we all have that one we never quite get over. The face you see in your dreams, the song that meant something to both of you that you find yourself singing when you reminisce, she's the one."

"Yes," said Jack. "She's the one."

"How long have you known her?" asked Keith, never having seen Jack so thoughtful before.

"We were teenagers together; she was going out with a school friend of mine. It took me a long time to approach her to tell her how I felt about her and when I did, she had become a bit of an obsession with me. I think I frightened her to death and, of course, she was not going to finish with her boyfriend for me. I don't know what I had been thinking about. I had nothing to offer her and her boyfriend was a trainee doctor at the time."

"So what happened?"

"She chose neither of us in the end but concentrated on her career and soon after I auditioned for the group so I never saw her again. She eventually did marry Ben but they divorced later. I don't think she ever married again."

"So you're both free to try again?"

"I doubt if it will be as easy as that. When I'm away on tour, so much a meaningful relationship is difficult to sustain."

"Some of us manage it."

"Yes, you have and very successfully, I admire you."

"I'm a very lucky man to have Elaine in my life."

"Yes, you are."

Chapter 7

Jack called me twice at the airport. I was introduced to each member of the band during these calls. There was Jay on drums, Keith on bass guitar and Adam on Keyboards. Each of them said hello as if we had known each other forever.

The first time Jack called, they were waiting to go on stage and in the background I could hear the noise of the audience. I asked Jack how many people were in the auditorium and he said he wasn't sure; it was usually between three and five thousand. I was incredulous. The second time he called, they were on a short break and I was amazed he had taken the time to speak to me.

"I can't wait to see you again," he said. "It seems unbelievable to have met this way so far from home."

My flight was called and we began boarding so I could not say anymore, however over the next few weeks we spoke every day, usually late at night. I don't think he stopped to think about the time difference, he just phoned and we talked about everything and nothing at the same time. He was always on a high after the performances and gushed about the venues, audiences and playlists. What had worked and what needed changing.

I learnt a lot about him, the band and his home life during those calls. I also made it my business to buy his records so I could familiarise myself with his work. I read back articles in music magazines to catch up on his success. I read interviews he had given and I became obsessed with finding out as much as I could about him. When he came home, I felt I knew a lot more about him and what I had read and listened to I liked.

He wanted me to meet him at the airport but that day I was in meetings all day with the Canadian Health Care group that was interested in setting up our clinics in Canada so it was impossible but as the next day was Friday, I booked the weekend off and we arranged to meet Friday evening. He had told me to bring a weekend case; he wanted me to stay the weekend.

At first, I was reluctant, it was too soon but then I thought, 'Hell, we have waited a long time for this why am I hesitating?'

A limousine called for me and I was driven to a small discreet little restaurant in a Cotswold village not far from where he lived.

The lighting in the room was low and although it was cosy and romantic, I couldn't see him at first. He was already there waiting for me at a table in the back of the room and as I walked in, his face lit up so pleased after all these weeks finally to be together again. I felt special and I suddenly wondered just how many of his fans would like to be standing in my shoes at that moment in time.

He took my hand and kissed me on the cheek.

"I can't believe you're actually here," he said, "I have waited so long."

"It's only been five weeks," I replied.

"No," he said. "To me, it's been a lifetime."

I laughed and he smiled, taking my hand. He was still holding and kissing my fingers.

Dinner was beautiful. The restaurant staff was so attentive. They all knew who he was, of course and seemed a little curious about me. I was not a typical pop star's girlfriend; I was not a young girl for a start; I was almost the same age as Jack, not a young flashy blond with long legs, plastic boobs and a tight short skirt. But I felt like a million dollars and Jack seemed so pleased we were together at last.

During the evening I began to understand why the table we were sat at was discreetly tucked away from the main body of the restaurant because once or twice during dinner when Jack was recognised people came over and asked for his autograph.

When we left the restaurant, there was a photographer waiting outside and suddenly flashbulbs were going off in our faces. I managed to put my small purse up over my face and Jack pulled me into the waiting car.

"Sorry about that," he said. "It's something you'll get used to, eventually."

Would I get used to it, I thought and what did he mean by, eventually? Was this going to be a long-term relationship? We drove away with all sorts of thoughts spinning around in my head.

He kissed me as we sat inside the limo. I felt like a teenager again, all nervous and apprehensive. I had butterflies in my stomach. Would he still feel the same about me after the weekend? Would I be a disappointment?

We drove for about fifteen minutes and eventually came to large black iron gates that opened automatically as we approached. The driveway was about a mile and a half long lined with established trees that seemed to form a canopy and when the house came into view, it was an Elizabethan manor house with a black and white façade and tall chimneys standing out against the starry moonlight sky.

The door of the car opened and I got out, Jack followed. "That's fine Charles, we won't be needing you anymore tonight," Jack said.

I wondered how many other women Charles had known arrived this way and be informed he would not be needed again that night. I felt a chill as I stood there. Just how foolish was I to think I was something special? This must be a regular occurrence. "What's the matter?" Jack asked. "Are you cold? Let's get you inside in the warm."

Two large oak doors opened into a huge wood-panelled hall that seemed to run the length of the front of the house. On the right-hand side was an open Tudor-style fireplace with a roaring fire. In front of us was a round highly polished table that would seat a considerable number of people if used as a dining table which sat on a pale blue rectangular rug. In the centre of the table was a cut-glass vase filled with long-stemmed white roses and mistletoe.

On the left-hand side rose a wide oak staircase which curved and formed a gallery landing on the next floor and from the ceiling hung a large Chrystal chandelier. Several doors faced us on the opposite side of the hall and on either side of the fireplace with a further door under the stairs, the door of which was slightly open. The hall was dimly lit and looked cosy and felt warm with the heat of the fire. I thought the whole of my little cottage would fit into this hall. So this is how a famous rock star chooses to live I thought.

At that moment, a small dark-haired woman appeared and took our coats from us. "Thank you, Edna," said Jack. "It's certainly warmer in here than outside tonight."

"Yes, Sir," Edna replied. "I've lit the fire in the sitting room and there's hot coffee waiting for you."

Jack took my hand and led me into a sitting room that was also panelled the same way as the hall. It made it seem dark but it was cosy. In this room was a large inglenook fireplace, which was lit and blazing away with what looked like half a tree burning in the grate. The space was filled with dark brown leather sofas and chairs. Heavy draped curtains covered the windows. On the coffee table was a tray with coffee cups and brandy glasses.

Jack took a cut-glass decanter from the side table and poured me a rather large brandy and then poured us both coffees.

"Are you not having a brandy?" I asked.

"No," he said. "I gave up drinking nine years ago. We all did as a band. After one of us died from a drug overdose, it was awake up call for us all and the way we were living. The first night I came off stage without having had a drink all day, I realised just how wonderful the experience had been. Instead of being in a drunken stupor, I had such clarity of the whole performance and I have rarely drank hard liquor since; in fact, it's banned from backstage when we're on tour. I have the occasional wine with dinner and a beer when the boys are around but that's about it. But you drink up, it will warm you up."

"I think this much will have me flat on my back. I don't know about warming me up," I replied.

"Well, I wouldn't mind that option either," he said, smiling.

I laughed and started to think I wouldn't mind it either.

"You have a beautiful house, how long have you lived here?" I asked.

"About ten years," he replied. "It was the biggest amount of money I have ever spent and even now I shake when I think about signing the cheque. I like it because it's private and it's very rare fans manage to get in. Would you like a tour?"

"Yes please," I replied, trying not to sound as nosey as I was feeling.

The downstairs consisted of a sitting room, dining room, study, kitchen, games room with a full-sized snooker table, breakfast room and staff quarters that I later learnt were occupied by Edna, the housekeeper, Charles the chauffeur having an apartment above the garages. In the cellar there was a bowling alley, cinema room and swimming pool complex and gym. There was a tunnel which led from here to the recording studio. This was detached from the main house and was a separate building in the grounds.

There were no windows in this room, all the walls were white and at one end there was a sound booth and the other a control room that looked a little bit like the console of the Star Ship Enterprise. Hanging on the walls were numerous framed platinum, gold and other discs. Guitars stood on stands all about the room. There were drums and other instruments all over the floor area, with a grand piano tucked into the far corner.

Jack started to describe the various different guitars but he must have noticed my eyes glaze over and he started to smile. "Too much information this time of night?" he asked.

"Sorry," I said.

"It's a bit of an obsession of mine. I forget not everyone is so enthralled."

He came over to me and took the glass I was still holding and placed it down on the floor. He put his arms around me and pulled me close to him, kissing me hard and passionately on the lips. His one hand unzipped my dress and it dropped effortlessly to the floor. He pulled his t-shirt over his head and kissed me again first on the lips then my neck and I felt his mouth kiss my body from my neck to my breasts, having swiftly removed my bra, he kissed my stomach and finally my groin. I groaned.

He pulled me down to the floor, removed the rest of our clothes and he was inside me with such a passion and vigour. Both of us breathing hard and fast, legs entwined. We climaxed together and held each other tightly until our breathing slowed.

Jack moved away from me but caught my hair in his watch as he did so.

"Oh," I said.

"Have I hurt you?" Jack asked, sounding concerned.

"No, you just caught my hair," I replied. "Although at my age I don't think a hard floor enhances the experience," I said smiling Jack started to laugh.

"No," he said. "I expect you're right; I just couldn't wait any longer. The next time, I'll make sure you're more comfortable."

"The next time?" I queried.

"Oh yes, the next time and the next and the next," he said, laughing.

"And what about your jet lag?" I asked.

"I think I have found the cure," he said.

We both started laughing then.

Chapter 8

He kept his word; the next time was in his comfy four poster bed. This time it was love-making, not just passionate sex. He was a considerate lover, making sure I was pleased as much as him. The experience lasted a long time and eventually Jack fell away from me, still breathing quite hard and quickly. I turned towards him and nestled my head in the crook of his shoulder.

The four-poster bed we were in was huge and hung with heavy tapestries on either side. It felt dark and depressing, not my idea of comfort at all. However, the size of the room was so big the bed took up so little space. Jack suddenly said, "I'm thirsty. Would you like a drink?"

"Yes please," I replied. "Just some water would be great."

"Nothing else? What about some chilled champagne?" he said.

"No water would be great, thanks."

He got out of bed and walked totally naked to the other side of the room. He seemed to have no shyness about displaying his body I was more of a prude about showing mine. He reached for a dressing gown and left. I pulled the bedclothes up around me and closed my eyes, feeling very sleepy.

The next thing I knew, his body was next to mine again and he was pulling me closer to him. Suddenly I realised he felt different and I turned around to lie on my back. As I looked up, I saw that the face above me was a perfect stranger.

"What the—?" was all I managed to say before a hand was put over my mouth.

"Shhhh, little lady," said a voice. "We're just going to have some fun." His breath smelled strongly of alcohol.

I did manage to pull my head away from the hand over my mouth and I screamed "Jack" as loud as I possibly could.

The hand that I had escaped from suddenly came down with such force and hit me at the side of my mouth. The searing pain was instant.

"You deserved that," the voice said. "I told you to be quiet, the more you resist, the more I shall enjoy the experience."

My jaw hurt. I was so frightened I couldn't believe this nightmare I suddenly found myself in. Jack, Jack, where are you? Why have you left me here like this? I thought to myself as I started to cry.

The man was astride on top of me, he was heavy and I could hardly breathe. I started to feel lightheaded and to lose consciousness.

Then I heard Jack's voice.

"What the bloody hell do you think you are playing at?" he shouted.

The man quickly moved off me and air filled my lungs again. I started to cough uncontrollably. I felt a woman's arms around me and realised that Jack's housekeeper, Edna, was in the room with us.

"Are you OK, Miss?" she asked solicitously.

I was still coughing, unable to speak.

"It's alright, Bruv," the man said. "The little lady and I were just having a bit of fun."

"Bruv?" I managed to squeak. "This is your brother?" I asked looking at Jack. "He was about to rape me. He hit me so hard; I should report him to the police."

"Oh come off it," the brother said. "You wanted it as much as I did. In fact, Bruv, she was begging me for it. You know what some of these fans are like, can't get enough, will go with anyone."

At that point, Jack slung a fist at him and hit him so hard, he fell backwards against the wall with some force.

"Get out of here and don't show your face in this house ever again," Jack said, spitting venom.

"Good riddance," said Edna. "It's about time you came to your senses about him."

The brother was rubbing his jaw where Jack's fist had just landed.

"This isn't over," he said.

"Oh yes, it is," said Jack. "I've told you for the last time, get out."

Then Jack said, "Wait," and the brother turned with a grin on his face, thinking that Jack had changed his mind already. "Your keys," Jack said, holding out his hand.

The brother's expression changed. He took keys from his pocket and threw them towards Jack. "Go to hell, all of you," he said as he turned and left.

Edna got up from my side and said she would make us a hot drink.

Jack came and sat beside me, putting his arm around me and drawing me towards him.

"Are you OK?" he said. "Did he hurt you? Oh my god, your mouth is bleeding."

I lifted my hand to my mouth and felt moisture. When I looked at my hand, there was blood on it.

"I was so frightened," I said, sobbing. "I couldn't breathe; I actually began to think I was going to die. Why would he do such a thing?" I asked.

"I don't know what's the matter with him," said Jack. "It's unbelievable that he should act in that way."

"He smelt of drink. Who is he?" I asked. "Is he really your brother?"

"Yes," said Jack. "Well, he's actually my Stepbrother, his name is Stephen. He's my mother's stepson from her first marriage but we have always been brought up as brothers."

"Well, I don't ever want to meet him again," I said. "In fact, I think he should be reported to the police because if that is his general behaviour, he's a dangerous man."

"Please don't," said Jack. "I will support you if you really want to do that and I know you have had a terrible experience but the backlash of publicity it would cause would be horrendous. I promise you, you will never have to come in contact with him again."

At that moment, Edna, the housekeeper, came back into the room with a tray of tea. She poured me a cup but when she saw my face, she said to Jack that perhaps he should call Doctor Janus as she didn't like the look of the gash on my face.

He immediately got up and made the call and Edna sat beside me.

It was not long after that a young doctor arrived. Jack explained to me that he was the doctor the group used when on tour. He took several minutes looking at my face, then asked Edna for some warm water and cotton wool. He explained to me that the gash would need some stitches but he was reluctant to do this himself as it was on my face and he did not want to leave me with a scar.

He took Jack to one side and they spoke quietly together for a few minutes. Doctor Janus came back to me and started cleaning the injury. He said he would temporarily seal the gash and make arrangements in the morning for me to see a friend of his who was a plastic surgeon to have it repaired without leaving a scar. He said he would give me something to take the pain away and help me sleep.

Jack looked ashen with worry. After the doctor had gone, he came and held me until I fell asleep.

The next morning I woke feeling as if I had gone several rounds with Mike Tyson. Jack came into the room and said Dr Janus had phoned and we had an appointment in two hours at the clinic. He asked if I needed any help getting ready, to which I replied I wasn't sure.

At that, he came over and put his arms around me and I thought for a moment he was about to cry.

"I am so sorry," he said. "I can't believe that I have allowed this to happen to you. That you may be scared for life and it's entirely my fault."

"Why is it your fault?" I asked. "Stephen did this, not you. Look, I am sure the surgeon will put everything right. I shall be as right as reign this time tomorrow. Now go and run me a shower and fetch my case so I can get dressed."

He smiled at me and I smiled back as best as I could, but it bloody hurt. I showered and dressed and when I came back into the room, there was coffee and toast waiting for me. I managed the coffee but was unable to chew anything so dipped the bread into the coffee until it was soggy enough to eat.

The surgeon was someone I knew, so that made me feel a little better. His name was James Ogden and in the past he had worked with Ben. He asked me what had happened and I explained it was an accident, but I am not sure he believed me and looked at Jack very suspiciously. I suddenly became aware of the type of publicity that would arise if the papers found out about this. Jack was right I could not report Stephen to the police.

In all, it took about two hours for James to repair the gash on my face. He said it would take several days before the bruising started to heal and several weeks before the flesh would eventually go back to look anything like normal. He gave me something to take for the pain, for which I was very grateful.

He told Jack I was to rest for several days and to bring me back in a week's time.

When we arrived back at Jack's, there was a lovely log fire burning in the grate and Edna had made soup for our lunch. I managed to sip the soup, which felt wonderful and as soon as I settled down on the big comfy sofa, I was fast asleep.

When I woke, it was dark and there was only the light from the fire. For a moment, I could not think where I was. Then the pain on the side of my face brought everything back to me.

"Dad," a girl's voice said. "Dad, she's awake. The lady's awake."

Jack was suddenly beside me, together with a young man who looked very much like him and a pretty young girl.

"OK, kids, let's give her some room to breathe," said Jack. "Turn the light on, Wills, will you?"

"Hi you," he said. "How are you feeling?"

I sat up and looked around at the faces all peering at me. "I'm OK I think," I said "Bit sore, could I have a drink of water so I can take one of my tablets?"

"I'll get it," said the young girl, dashing out of the room. She looked about thirteen years of age, quite tall certainly considerably taller than me, very pretty with long dark waist length hair and large dark eyes that seemed to twinkle when she smiled, returning very quickly with a glass of water and Edna who was holding a tray laden with all sorts of teatime goodies.

"I have liquidised some food for you, madam, in case you were still having problems eating," she said.

"That is so good of you, Edna," I said. "I think I might be eating through a straw for some time."

Jack handed me the glass of water and put one of the tablets James had given me into my hand.

"Do you know you snore?" said the young girl.

"Chrissy, don't be so rude," said Wills. He reminded me so much of the young Jack I used to know. He was also tall and dark but very handsome and I guessed about 17 years of age. The children both turned heads but seemed at ease with their looks there was no showing off or feeling of privilege about either of them.

"No," I replied. "I didn't know I snored no one has ever told me before."

"It's not too bad, not as bad as dad," she said. "I'm Chrissy, by the way and that's my brother William. It's Wills for short."

"Hello, Chrissy and Wills, how very nice to meet you both," I said.

"Hello," was the reply from both of them.

"OK, that's enough now," said Jack. "Let's leave the nice lady to sip her coffee, you can come back later," said Jack.

"How are you?" Jack asked.

"My face feels sore," I replied. "But I feel fine. How long have I been asleep?"

"About five hours."

"I hope I didn't snore the whole time," I said jokingly.

Jack laughed, "She is very good at saying things just how they are," he said.

"It's refreshing to find someone so honest."

"Oh, she's that alright, too much too honest at times."

After I had eaten, the children came back in and the television was turned on and we all settled down for a couple of hours. Chrissy asked numerous questions very directly and in the end Jack told her to stop as I looked as if I was getting a headache.

I had begun to feel sleepy again; it must have been the tablets. Jack said he would take me up to bed. He said he would sleep in the spare room so as I was not disturbed. But I said no, as I felt uncomfortable and uneasy about being left alone. The events of last night had left a bad impression on me and it was a long time before I ever felt good being by myself in the house again.

I slept late on Sunday morning and after showering and getting dressed, Wills brought a tray of coffee and toast.

"I can bring you more to eat if you are hungry," he said, placing the tray on the bed. "But lunch is at 1 o'clock today as both Chrissy and I have to be back at school by five."

"Your dad says you board during the week. Do you enjoy that?" I asked.

"I don't mind, but Chrissy isn't so keen, she misses being at home," Wills replied. "It's just more convenient with dad away so much."

"Thank you for the coffee, it's just what I needed," I said.

"You're welcome," he replied, smiling.

Within moments of him leaving, Jack came into the room. "How are you?" he asked. "Is your face still hurting?"

"It's a lot better, thank you," I replied. "I removed the dressing whilst I was in the shower. It's still red but it doesn't hurt so much."

"I can't get over the feeling that you may be left with a scar and it's my entire fault because I have allowed Stephen free access to this house."

"Well, he's gone now, so let's not think about it anymore."

"I'm so sorry," he said and kissed me gently on the forehead.

There was a knock on the door and Jack said, "Yes, come in."

It was Edna. "There's a telephone call for you, madam, a gentleman by the name of Amos."

"Thank you, Edna," I said.

"You can take it at the bedside," Jack said.

"Thanks, I left your number as you suggested. Excuse me."

"Hello, Amos, how are you?" I said, answering the phone.

"I'm fine," he replied. "Are you enjoying your weekend?"

"Yes," I said, touching the dressing on my face.

"I'm calling because I've heard from the Canadian's," he said. "They want to meet us Tuesday morning with a proposal. Can you make that?"

"Yes, of course," I said. "What time do you want me?"

"Well, they're arriving at eleven but I need to speak to you first," he said. "Can we meet for breakfast about 8:30? What I have to discuss will make a difference to our response to their proposal, whatever it is they are going to say."

I was intrigued. Amos had been so enthusiastic about this development and now he suddenly sounded apprehensive.

"Yes, of course, that's fine," I said. "I'll see you at the clinic at 8:30."

As I put the phone down, Jack must have noticed I looked a bit puzzled.

"What's up?" he asked.

"Not sure," I replied. "Amos wants to discuss something with me on Tuesday morning before meeting this Canadian company. He sounded serious."

"I was hoping you could stay longer," Jack said.

"I'm sorry, but this meeting is important for the future of the business. We've been in discussions with them for months."

"How about if I come with you to London?" he asked. "I've something I could do whilst I'm there and at least we could have our evenings together."

"Well, if you want to," I replied. "I won't have any time during the day, though."

"I'll book us a hotel and I'll drive us down on Monday evening," he said.

"No need, we can stay at the flat," I said. "Are you sure it's OK with you? You won't be bored?"

"I want to and we can be back by Friday in time for you to see Doctor Janus."

"OK, as long as you are sure."

We spent the rest of the day with the children and when the time came for them to leave, I suggested to Jack that we take them back to school. I felt like a drive and getting out of the house. I was starting to get cabin fever.

As we were driving, I discussed with Jack the plans the Canadian company was making with us. He asked if it would mean me being away from home more often and I said yes either myself or Amos we usually shared the workload equally between us.

Jack asked if Amos was married and had a family, to which I smiled.

I said "No, he's not married but he has a partner of long standing. His name is John Cutler. He's one of our consultant psychiatrists."

"Oh," said Jack, immediately understanding a little bit more about my business partner.

"Now that we have met again," said Jack. "I was hoping we would be able to spend more time together. I know it's selfish of me but I don't want to let you go. You could give up work, you know, I could look after you."

"I have worked long and hard to get where I am Jack, so has Amos. I could not just walk away even if I wanted to."

"I know," he said. "I have no right to ask, but I couldn't bear to lose you again."

Making love that night was really special. Jack made me feel like I was the only women he had ever been with, which, of course, was not the case. He had told me about the band's hedonistic early years. How fame had gone to their heads. The drinking, drugs and girls were all provided by their management to keep them performing and happy.

Jack said it was easy to take everything that was being offered but after the first three years of being constantly on the road touring from one end of the country to the other they discovered as a band they were broke. The money that they had been earning was being taken by everyone but them.

They wised up and got new management and a different recording company and stopped being ripped off. This also coincided with the death of one of their group by a drugs overdose so as a band the drinking and drugs use stopped. Jack also started dating Marie again and stopped sleeping around. The band grew up and concentrated on their music and success.

Chapter 9

The following morning, after breakfast, Jack drove me home. I needed to pack a suitcase and pick up papers needed for Tuesday's meeting. He also wanted to see where I lived. He immediately made himself at home, investigated each room and petted my two little kittens, that were so pleased to see us both.

"I love this," said Jack. "It's so cosy and it looks Christmassy with the tree already up and decorated. You will have to do the tree at home for the kids. I've never thought of having one before."

"Really?" I asked. "The hallway is an ideal place for one."

"Can we do one next weekend? Chrissy will love to decorate it," Jack asked. "If we have time, we can shop for decorations whilst we're in London."

"I'm not sure I will be free next weekend," I said. "I may need to work on this proposal that is going to be put to Amos and myself tomorrow."

"Can't you work on it at my place?" he asked. "I tour again at the end of February and I just want to spend as much time with you as possible before then. I hoped we could spend Christmas together."

"Jack, all this is so sudden," I said. "I have a life that's full of friends and colleagues, work and patients whose treatment is only partially completed. There is a time when I take my turn being on call for any emergencies that arise from work. You're asking me to step out of my life and step in to yours. I can't do that."

"No, of course not," he answered, looking crestfallen. "I get so caught up in what I want, I forget people have their own lives. You see, my life is so full and exciting I can't imagine why anyone wouldn't want to be part of it. How egotistical is that?"

"Mmm, quite," I said, smiling at him.

"Look," I said. "I'm not saying I don't want to be a part of your life, I do, but this is all so sudden. We haven't discussed anything about how we feel about each other or where we want this relationship, if there is a relationship, to go. I think we need to slow down and just enjoy getting to know each other again."

"You're right, of course," he said. "I know I feel the same about you the way I always have. We have spent so long apart, I want to fill every moment we now have. I'll try not to push you into anything but I'm very used to getting my own way and people giving in to my every wish."

"You'll most probably be very disappointed with me then," I said.

"Never," he replied, pulling me close to him and kissing me hard and very passionately on the neck. We made love there and then, to the amusement of the cats who watched, intrigued by the goings on.

We travelled down to the flat at Chelsea Harbour after lunch and arrived about four o'clock. The flat which was in the Belvedere tower was very different to my little thatched country cottage. I had decorated this all white with glass coffee tables and steel light fittings. It was modern but still feminist and cosy.

"How long have you had this flat?" Jack asked.

"I bought it after Ben and I divorced," I answered. "I was spending more and more time in London with the business and clinics that I thought I would invest in a flat rather than spend my time in hotels. It turned out to be a good investment."

"I love the views," he said.

"I've booked us into the Chelsea Harbour hotel for dinner," I said. "I don't have much in the fridge. I'll do a shop tomorrow."

"I'm not very good at being out in public, especially in London I hate being recognised and the press being so invasive," he said.

"Oh, don't worry about that here. There are so many celebrities that live on this complex no one takes much notice," I re-assured him.

He still wore his dark glasses into the restaurant and didn't remove them until halfway through the second course.

I left Jack at the flat the following morning as I left just after 7:30 to get to the clinic by the appointed time. The place was as usually busy and I was handed a pile of messages. I took myself off to the room we used as a boardroom and found Amos there already with coffee and assorted pastries.

"My goodness," he said. "What's happened to your face? Have you been in an accident?"

I was about to say I had been in an accident but Amos and I had always promised to be honest and up front with each so I told him exactly what had happened.

"Are you mad?" he asked. "You must inform the police, he can't get away with this."

"That's what I wanted to do at first," I replied. "But the press would soon be on it and they would feature Jack more so than his brother. I don't want the press recognition yet and I didn't think the publicity would be welcomed by the Canadians."

"Are you absolutely sure?" he asked. "I doubt if he hasn't done this before."

"Well, Jack's banned him from the house and he has been warned that if he tries to contact me again, he will lose the job he has as road manager with the band. I don't think he will risk losing that."

"I don't know if I'm going to like this Jack of yours."

"Oh you will," I said. "Because I do."

"OK, if you say so. Here, have a coffee and one of your favourite chocolate croissants," he said, smiling at me but still looking concerned.

"You certainly know how to get to a girl's heart," I said, biting a rather large piece of croissant.

After a few moments, I asked, "So what's this meeting about? What's happened?"

"You don't miss much do you? But you need to know that my circumstances and priorities have changed and I feel I can no longer support the commitment that will be needed to open clinics in Canada," he said.

"What? Why?" I asked. "You were so keen on moving forward. You and John were even thinking about moving to Canada. What's changed?"

"It's John," he replied very quietly looking down at the floor. "He's been diagnosed with cancer of the oesophagus."

"Oh my God, Amos," I said, "How bad is it?"

"Well, they think they have caught it early, but it is going to need chemo and if the tumour shrinks, it will need surgery then more chemo. It's going to be a long haul and I want to be with him every step of the way."

"Of course, you do," I said, feeling absolutely devastated. They were such a together couple I could not imagine one of them without the other.

"Look, it's not the end of the world," I said after a few moments. "This is not something we were actually seeking, they approached us after all. We can just carry on with the business as it is. It's successful, we earn a good amount of money from it, more than either of us need and I can manage if you need time off. It's fine, we're adaptable and John has to be both of our priority now."

"Are you sure?" he asked. "I thought I was letting you down. This deal seemed to be the pinnacle of our success. It's everything we ever wanted."

"Well, if the truth be known, I thought lately we were taking on more work than perhaps we envisaged or really wanted. There would never have been time for a personal life or time to enjoy the success we have already achieved. It's a terribly reason not to go forward but in some respects perhaps we should have stopped and asked ourselves if it was what we really wanted."

"I thought you would be disappointed," he said. "We've both been so ambitious about building the business. How come you are just accepting this?"

"I'm not," I replied. "But thinking how quickly things change and how fleeting life is at all, perhaps I can see that there are other things to life, not just success and money. You know I have been so busy with the business that I can't remember the last meaningful relationship I had. Don't get me wrong, I have loved every moment of it but it doesn't love you back, does it? It doesn't hold you close in the middle of the night, frightening the beasts away and whispers I love you in your ear."

"My, he must be something, this Jack of yours," Amos said.

"Yes, I think he is," I replied.

In the end, it was not that decision we had to make. Talk about getting something absolutely wrong. The Canadian company did want to build clinics in Canada-based on our business ethics but they wanted to buy the clinics we already had, this would be the three in the UK and the one in America. The clinics would remain in our name and Amos and I would keep 10% share between us. We would not be unable to sell our stake for five years or open other businesses in our names.

We would still be able to practice but only in the clinics themselves as Directors or in any practice that was already established. There were a lot more whys and wherefores but basically that was the proposal except for the amount of money they were offering each of us. If we signed on the bottom line, we would be 40 million dollars each better off over the next five years.

To say we were both stunned was an understatement. After hearing this, we said we needed time to discuss it and the Canadians gave us to the weekend to come back to them.

When they left, we both sat in the boardroom, speechless.

"I need a drink," said Amos, going to the cabinet and pouring us both a shot of whiskey, not sure why as it was neither of our tipple, but we both took a large gulp just the same.

"Can you believe that?" I said. "I didn't see that coming, did you?"

"Never," said Amos. "Forty million. Are they serious?"

"So it would seem," I said, taking another gulp of the whisky.

We looked at each other and started laughing. We laughed so loudly that Joanne, our secretary, came in to ask if everything was alright.

"Yes, we're fine, Joanne, just a bit hysterical," said Amos, which started me off again. Joanne went out and Amos and I finally calmed down.

"I need to talk to John about this," said Amos. "He was really concerned about how it was going to go today. I have to tell him, he'll be incredulous."

Amos left the room to telephone John in private and I sat there with a thousand thoughts going round in my head. What now? I thought. Life certainly throws you a curve ball when you least expect it.

Joanne returned with some fresh coffee.

"I'm just going out for some lunch," she said. "Can I get you or Amos anything?"

"No, thank you, Joanne," I replied. "I think we will be leaving soon."

"How about some lunch?" asked Amos, coming back into the room?

"Yes, let's go," I said. "I think I could do with some air."

We talked endlessly over lunch about every aspect of the morning not coming to any conclusion at all and finally decided to go away, clear our heads and meet tomorrow afternoon. I didn't have any appointments that day so I made my way back to the flat, stopping to shop for groceries on the way. Jack was still out when I got back so I decided to go and have a long hot soak in the bath to try and gather my thoughts.

I had started supper by the time he arrived back and by the time he had washed and changed, supper was on the table.

He asked me how the meeting had gone, but I didn't want to go into the detail with him so I just said that the proposal was significant to the future of the business and we both needed some time to consider what it meant to us both. I did tell him, though, about what Amos had told me about John and his illness.

"Will that mean more work for you if Amos wants time off?" he asked.

"I have said that I will support him in any way that he needs," I replied. "But I am sure we can work things out. Although it is very much a two-man business, we have plenty of people that will be willing to step up and help. We can also employ some locums; it's not the end of the world."

"If there is anything I can do to help, just let me know," he said. "I want to be part of your life now. You're important to me."

"Thanks," I said, suddenly realising how important he was becoming to me too.

Chapter 10

I didn't sleep well. I tossed and turned until the early hours and finally got up and made myself a fruit tea drink. I sat in the chair by the window, watching London change from night to day. The capital was still lit up and the noises of traffic and the occasional emergency vehicle made the city seem a different place to the way it was during the day.

I loved sitting here and having the time just to look, which was very rare. I realised if I wanted this time to myself, it could become more a way of life if Amos and I sold out. Would I enjoy that? I know recently work was becoming a burden to be got through each day rather than a joy. I did not seem to have time to do the things that were important to me. I missed not spending time with my friends, they would phone me and say they were meeting for coffee or lunch but I was never free.

Since Mom had died, I had spent little time with dad and although he never mentioned it to me, I know we both would like to see more of each other. Also, the last few days with Jack had made me realise just how much my life was a void of anything but work.

It felt good being held and kissed, laughing and talking the day over with someone who was interested enough to ask. There had been other relationships since Ben but they had ended because I didn't have time to nurture them and give up enough time to invest in being in someone else's life. I didn't want that to happen with Jack. I realised suddenly just how much I was missing these everyday ordinary things.

"What's up?" It was Jack's voice. "Can't you sleep?" he asked.

"No, my mind is too busy," I replied. "I'm sorry. I didn't mean to disturb you."

"You didn't," he said. "I woke up and just missed you."

He came over and put his arms around me. "Come back to bed," he said. "Let me make you feel better."

So I did and he did.

In the space of a few days, my life changed considerably. Amos and John decided that with John's diagnosis their priority was to spend as much time together as they possibly could and I decided I did not want to take on the extra workload. I was tired, I needed a rest. So we sold out to the Canadians, with neither of us regretting it at all.

We had successfully built up the business from nothing so there was no need to feel like failures. We both had enough money to make our futures secure and if we wanted to go on and practice, we still could. I still had my writing career and would now have more time to write. I had time for myself, do whatever I wanted and I realised I wanted Jack. I did not inform him of my decision until after it was all signed and finalised. He was surprised but delighted as well. He could not believe the amount of money involved in the sale and I think he was a bit disappointed that this meant I would be financially independent.

With very few amendments, Amos and I signed the provisional agreement on the Thursday afternoon and Jack and I drove home on Thursday night. There was a late-night supper waiting for us plus loads of deliveries of Christmas decorations that I discovered Jack had spent his time buying in London. Jack said he would like to throw a party for both of our friends and families. He said he wanted everyone to know we were a couple and that we were both happy.

So, we started to make plans to have a New Year's Eve party, Invites were sent out, extra help was hired to help Edna with the catering and extra security for Charles the chauffeur to organise. Chrissy and Wills helped me decorate the tree and the house (Jack seemed to go missing) and they both looked forward to having their friends at the party, although we did have to cut down on their lists.

During this time I was also going backwards and forwards from my own home and work so by the time Christmas Eve arrived I was weary and unbelievably tired to say the least but I still enjoyed every minute of the festive season. Jack insisted that dad came and stayed with us for Christmas and he took to Jack and the children right away.

Lying in bed very late on Christmas Eve, Jack noticed how tired I was looking and realised just how much he had been expecting of me.

"I'm sorry," he said. "I've been very selfish, as usual. I've turned your life upside down and got caught up in all the excitement because I've been so happy. You have been so busy dealing with the business, negotiating with the staff and the new owners; I haven't noticed how much pressure I have put on you preparing for my family Christmas. I'm so sorry."

"Well, I am tired, but that doesn't mean I haven't enjoyed every minute of it," I replied. "I want the children to enjoy this Christmas because next year Wills will be at university and perhaps you won't all be together like this again."

"I hadn't thought of that," he said. "After the new year, perhaps when the children go back to school, if you can get the time, let's take a holiday and just lie on the beach somewhere enjoying each other's company."

"That sounds absolutely wonderful," I replied.

Christmas was wonderful. Edna even allowed me to help with the cooking. Chrissy was so excited by the time Christmas morning arrived she was physically sick before lunch was served. We opened presents first thing in the morning still in our nightwear eating bacon sandwiches whilst sitting on the floor around the extremely large Christmas tree Jack had bought for the hall.

I don't know where all the presents came from. Jack bought me the most beautiful necklace with a heart and single diamond inside. There was an inscription on the inside of the rim of the heart which read 'You have my heart now and forever' which when I read it brought a tear to my eye. Wills was surprised to have just an envelope from me but his delight on opening it was just what I hoped for.

"What is it?" asked his dad.

"A week's work experience with a surgeon at the hospital. I could not ask for anything better," he said.

"Will you have to see people being cut open?" asked Chrissy.

"I hope so," said Wills. "If this is my chosen career, I need to experience what I am letting myself in for."

"I think you will make a wonderful doctor," said my dad.

I smiled, happy to know I had chosen the right thing.

Edna and Charles joined us for lunch. Neither seemed to have family to go to, although I learnt that Edna had two weeks off in January and spent them with her sister, who lived in Bournemouth. Dad loved every moment with the children and acted like a proper Grandfather, endlessly playing games with Chrissy with such patience and tolerance.

I was reminded how Christmas used to be when I was a little girl. I finally relaxed and eventually slept most of Boxing Day. Nobody seemed to mind and in the afternoon, we all wrapped up and went for a walk in the woods that surrounded the property. The wind was bitterly cold and I was glad my ears were covered, although everyone laughed at the silly Christmas woolly Santa hat I had chosen to wear.

We took Jack's two Labrador dogs with us and they bounded about as if they were having a happy Christmas as well. When we arrived back at the house, it started to snow so Christmas seemed complete, even the weather behaved just as we could have wished.

As I looked through the window, I remembered that evening long ago looking at Jack's footprints in the snow walking away from me and felt that I never wanted to see that again. Edna made a warm mulled wine that even Chrissy was allowed a sip of and we sat by the roaring fire, contented with life.

The next big event was the New Year's Eve party. I have never met so many famous people, although after a while I realised that most of them or their families had at some time been patients at the clinics. Success certainly brings its own problems.

The caterers arrived and there was so much food and drink, Chrissy was again sick and missed most of the fun having to go to bed early. I took her upstairs and tucked her in, she was asleep in seconds and Edna arrived with a bowl to put beside her bed. She had obviously experienced this type of event before.

"I see you've made yourself at home. Got your feet well under the table," said a voice that sent a chill to my very core. I looked round to see Stephen stood just inside the door holding a bottle of Jack Daniels whiskey in his hand.

Edna immediately stood between us. "You're not welcome here, Mr Stephen," she said. "You were told never to come to this house again. What are you doing here?"

"Oh, come off it, you know Jack didn't mean it. I'm his brother and I'm his family," he said, looking at me insinuating I had no status here. "You don't think he would pick some women over me, do you? I'm here to stay so you better get used to it."

He turned and left. I suddenly realised I was shaking. I found him so intimidating.

"Are you alright, madam?" asked Edna.

"Yes, I'm fine; I think I need to speak to Jack. Do you think he knows Stephen is here?"

"I don't know, madam. He was adamant Stephen was not to come here again," Edna replied.

She stayed with Chrissy for a while whilst I went downstairs to look for Jack.

At first I could not see him anywhere, so many people stopped me and complimented me on the house, the decorations, the food and it became an obstacle course trying to fight my way through the people. Then I saw him in the conservatory with Stephen. Their voices were raised and Jack looked so angry. I could not hear everything that was being said but I heard Stephen saying, "You owe me, you know you do."

"I owe you nothing, I have everything I have because I have worked for it and achieved my success on my own merit," Jack replied.

"It should have been mine," said Stephen. "You stole it from me, you know you did."

"Don't be so ridicules," replied Jack. "You constantly state I stole my success from you but it was never yours to take. You had already failed the audition before I was asked to audition and they liked me. I was successful on my own merit. I fitted in with what the band was looking for you didn't. It's as simple as that. I owe you nothing. In fact, you have had more from me that you have ever been entitled to. Now get out and don't come back."

"You'll regret this, Jack," said Stephen with venom in his voice. "I'm not going to take this lying down."

With these words, Stephen left. Jack stood silent for a little while, trying to compose himself and eventually leaving to re-join the party.

As I walked back through the hallway, everyone I met seemed to want to speak to me and whilst I smiled and joined in the general banter, I was still shaking inside. I was so frightened about bumping into Stephen, I felt panic rising inside me.

"Hey, what's the matter?" It was Amos. "You look awful."

"I'm OK. I just need to find Jack. Have you seen him?"

"No, here, sit down for a minute; you look as white as a ghost."

"Thanks, I'm OK; I just really need to speak to Jack."

At that moment Jack came into view, he had been speaking to Edna and as he saw me, he came over.

"It's OK, he's gone," he said on approaching us. "He knows not to come here again. I've told him he would lose his job if he came here again and as far as I am concerned that's what has happened. I want nothing more to do with him and if he comes here again, the police will be called."

"I hope that doesn't make him desperate," I said. "He doesn't seem the most compliant of people."

"I don't want you to be frightened about being here. I want you to feel safe in this house, that's the most important thing to me," Jack said. "I will do everything in my power to make sure that happens."

"Thanks Amos, I'll look after her now," Jack said to Amos. "Let's all go and enjoy the party, don't let him spoil our New Year."

I smiled. Jack was right we should not let Stephen spoil things for us. The party continued with everyone enjoying themselves. There seemed to be a crescendo of noise, laughter and music.

During the evening, Keith, the band's bass player and his wife, Elaine, asked if they could speak to me privately.

"It's about our son John," said Elaine. "For some time, in fact, since he was about 13, he has had a problem with drugs."

"At first he smoked some cannabis at school, then it escalated to hard drugs," said Keith. "We tried everything to get him some help and eventually he went into rehab. It was something he wanted and it was quite successful. For almost two years, he was absolutely clean."

"But now he's back on drugs, we think he's injecting heroin," said Elaine becoming tearful. "If he doesn't stop, we're frightened he's going to die. He's our only child we need some help."

"How old is he?" I asked.

"He's 19," said Keith.

"Does he want to stop?" was my next question to them.

"He's begging us to help him," said Keith. "He says he just can't help himself."

"I can't promise I can do anything for him," I said. "We are really busy at the moment, but I will see him. Can you bring him to the clinic after the holidays?"

"Yes, anything you can do would be wonderful. Thank you so much," said Elaine.

"Write your telephone number down here and I will find some appointment time and let you know where and when," I said. "He has to really want this if I am to be any help. You do understand that, don't you?"

"Yes, thank you," said Elaine, shaking my hand.

"Thank you," said Keith.

"Now, let's get back to the party," I said. "And try to smile. I promise I will do all I can."

I noticed on re-entering the hallway that Wills was being his charming self, all the young girls hanging on his every word. One or two people misbehaved but it was part of the party events. There was music with some of the guests 'Jamming' but of course they were entertainers so it's what they did best. It was the early hours of the morning before everyone had left and Jack and I fell into bed exhausted but glad things had been a success.

By the time we awoke the following morning, we were met by a host of people getting the house back to normal. There was a breakfast brunch set out for anyone that was still around, which seemed to be most of Will's friends who had appetites that could only be marvelled at. By early evening, the house seemed quiet again and life got back to normal if life with a rock star was ever normal.

Marie decided she wanted to see the children. It was the first we had heard from her since before Christmas but as usual she had to be obeyed and with some reluctance from both Wills and Chrissy Jack took them to London to meet her. Dad and I took the opportunity to go back to my cottage. He chose this rather than going back home because he had an old pal called Victor in the village that he was quite close to, so he came to stay with me to catch up with him.

It was during this time we managed to talk about his future. I was aware that the family house dad still lived in was too big for him and had started to become difficult for him to manage, the garden alone was over an acre and dad had started to employ a gardener to keep it in some sort of order. I broached the subject of him selling up and buying something smaller and easier to manage. I thought this would be met with a resounding 'no' but to my surprise he was quite agreeable.

Victor lived within a sheltered housing complex which dad had decided he liked and him and Victor thought they would like to have an allotment together. They also wanted to join the local green bowling club. It was something they enjoyed years ago when both their wives were alive and as each of them were still active, it was something they wanted to try again. The only drawback was dad living too far away. So with very little further discussion, dad's house went up for sale and a small one-bedroom property was purchased in the sheltered housing complex.

Dad seemed to find a second lease of life and he became so busy with Victor it was very difficult for him to find time for me. I was pleased he was happy although dealing with the sale and purchase of the properties and the clearance of all the furniture added to my already heavy workload. Luckily enough Jack and I found time for a holiday and we jetted off to the Caribbean for some well-needed rest which was a godsend because when I came home my feet barely touched the ground.

Amos took time off to be with his partner John, who had started a gruelling round of chemotherapy. Even after the first treatment, he started to lose his hair and by the time the third treatment began, even his eyebrows had gone. He was constantly nauseous and sick but the oncologist altered the drug mix and he slightly improved but it was a case of the treatment being worse than the symptoms of the decease itself.

Amos looked ill with anxiety and I started to fear for his health, but seeing a loved one deteriorate in front of your eyes is heart breaking. Several of Amos's clients started to see me instead, increasing my already heavy workload, which left me most of the time living at the flat in London.

I decided to take on Keith's son, John, as a patient. I liked the lad and he really did seem to want to get clean. He was sent to one of our clinics away from home and there were instructions that he could not have any family contact for twelve weeks. I think his parents found this very hard but they agreed to it and John's treatment began in earnest.

There were further negotiations with the Canadian group that had to be finalised, staff contracts that had to be re-negotiated and with Amos and myself taking a step back from the day-to-day management, new staff had to be employed to take over.

Luckily enough, the Canadian group had people they wanted to place in the roles that needed to be filled but the changeover was hectic and time consuming. There were days when I did not see Jack and he filled his time in the studio working on a new album, but we spent hours on the phone talking to each other. I really missed him very much and felt a bit out on a limb on my own but was too exhausted most of the time to think about it.

It was the second weekend in February that I managed to get back to the cottage. I arrived early in the day on Friday, knowing I did not have to be back in London until Wednesday morning the following week.

My cats came running to me as soon as I stepped through the door. I was surprised they recognised me I spent so much time away from them I was so lucky to have such a good neighbour that looked after them for me. The cottage looked so unfamiliar but after I had made a cup of tea and sat down for a few minutes, I started to relax and feel more at home. Within a few minutes, the phone started to ring which was good because I think I had started to dose off.

"Hello, what are you doing?" asked Jack.

"Well, I was just dosing off, so I am glad you rang as I have a lot to do," I replied.

"Well, don't bother cooking anything, I'm coming over to take you out this evening. I've missed you so much."

"That would be lovely, but do you know what I would really like?"

"Go on, tell me, but don't ask me to give you some time and space, I don't think I could."

"How about a take away and supper by the fire, just the two of us?" I suggested.

"That sounds great, I'll bring the food. See you about six if that's OK?"

"See you then, I must get on. Speak to you later."

"OK, bye, love you," he said and he was gone.

It made me feel better knowing I was going to see Jack this evening, so feeling revitalised, I began the many chores to be completed whilst I was home. Before long, the washing machine was on, the mountain of correspondence opened and dealt with and I showered and changed. By the time Jack arrived, the cottage was warm and cosy and the perfect setting for a romantic dinner.

"Hi," he said, coming through the door, loaded up with bags of food. "I have missed you so much." He put the bags down and put his arms around me, kissing me passionately on the lips.

"I've missed you too," I said, noticing that he smelt a little of Chinese food.

He kissed me again. It felt so good.

"I forgot to ask you what you would like to eat so I've bought a selection," he said, picking up the food and carrying it into the kitchen.

"Yes," I said smiling. "I can see. It looks like you bought the whole menu."

So we ate, we talked, laughed and caught up with each other's news.

"You look tired," he said. "You're dealing with too much on your own. Is there nothing I can do to help?"

"Not really," I replied. "It's mostly business stuff, but I would think over the next month as the new staff settle in, it will be easier. A lot of the therapy sessions are coming to an end as well and I don't intend to take on any new patients for the time being. I want the new regime to settle in and start taking over. I have told them that I want to act in a consultancy role only and take some time off to myself."

"I'm glad," Jack said. "And although I feel totally selfish, I want to spend more time with you. I can't help feel we have spent too long apart, there's a lot of time to make up for but I don't want to put any pressure on you as I know you're dealing with so much at the moment with work, your dad's move and Amos and John's problems."

"I feel the same," I said. "For the first time, I realise I need a better work life balance and if anything, John's illness has shown me that life is too short not to make the most of every moment. I want to spend more time with you too; it's been a long time since I had someone I wanted to make my life with. After my breakup with Ben, I concentrated on work and ignored everything else in my life but I'm tired. For the first time in my life, I am really tired. I realise I've achieved so much and perhaps it's time to start enjoying what I have been working for."

"I'm glad," said Jack. "It makes what I want to ask you a little easier. I tour for two months at the end of this month in the UK and Europe but when I come home, I would like you to move in with me. I know what I'm asking you to give up but I would like us to make a life together and living together would be the first step towards this."

"My, I wasn't expecting that," I said, quite taken aback.

"Look, I know it's a big ask but I love you and I want to spend my time with you. I have not felt this happy in years. Please say you will think about it?"

"Yes, of course, I will. I love you too. You don't think all this is too soon?" I asked.

"No," he said. "The more I think about it, the more I know it's right. It's exactly what I want."

Chapter 11

Being with Jack over the next few days was wonderful. We didn't do anything particularly exciting, just spent time being together. We spent a lot of time just relaxing in the cottage by a blazing open fire. We also walked for hours, although the weather had turned cold, but we wrapped up and huddled together.

Jack seemed at home in the cottage, although it was small and he seemed to fill the space completely. He said he wished his house felt as cosy as the cottage and asked if I did move in, would I like to change the décor so that I felt it was more like my home. I thought he would mind about having changes made but he said no. Very little had been done since he had moved in even most of the furniture was bought with the house and after being in the cottage and the flat in London, he realised the house was dark and dated.

He also wanted to update the staff quarters which badly needed doing, so we set down some ideas and plans and without saying yes, I would move in it all seemed to be happening without any more discussion.

In the end, as always with Jack, a few alterations became almost a full rebuilding event. There was very little of the original rooms which remained untouched. I had my own little sitting room come study, which was the unused breakfast room with new windows installed that opened into the garden. There was a new kitchen installed, the bedrooms were revamped, the master bedroom becoming light and airy with the fourposter bed consigned to the main guest room.

I had my own walk in dressing room designed and we had a new bathroom fitted to the master suite. Will's had a study added to his bedroom as we thought he would need his quiet space to work with his entrance to university looming and Chrissy's pink little girls' room became a teenage haven which she loved.

Edna's quarters were updated with a new bathroom and Charles' dated apartment over the garages had a new kitchen and bathroom. By the time Jack returned from his tour, most of the work was finished and he said it looked like a new house.

Of course, he missed all the upheaval, which the rest of us coped with whilst he was away. I decided to keep the cottage and rent it out. The biggest emotional event for me was moving my two little cats in. For the first few days, they spent their time hiding in every tiny space they could find but with Chrissy's coaxing and love they eventually settled down even making friends (sort of) with Jack's two dogs.

All through this, Edna was a brick. She coped with all the dust and comings and goings, smoothing the way for my move in. I sat down with her during this time and discussed how she felt having a woman in the house again and learnt that she had been worried about her role but I told her as far as I was concerned, the running of the house would still be hers and I just wanted to support her rather than take over something that was working very well.

So with very little hassle, I became a member of the London family household and felt everyone went out of their way to make me welcome and at home.

Having my home life organised for me, (With Edna it was suddenly like having a wife) my working life seemed to be easier. During the summer I had to spend a week in Canada discussing opening two new clinics, but Jack and the children and dad joined me and we spent a week touring the Rockies before flying down to Las Vegas for five days where Jack and the Testators were playing in one of the major casinos.

It was most probably the last time we would have a family holiday altogether because Wills would probably want to holiday with friends in future when he started university. We saw shows, had a helicopter ride over the Grand Canyon and did all the other touristy things there were to do.

Dressing for dinner one night, Jack asked if the dress I was wearing was new.

"Yes, do you like it?" I asked.

"Yes, I do, although like everything else you wear, it looks better in a heap on the floor."

I smiled; this was something Jack said very often. Jack walked over and kissed me.

"Did I hear Chrissy call you Mom today?" he asked.

"Yes," I replied. "I think she does it without thinking, I haven't picked her up on it and I don't want to make it an issue. Do you mind?"

"Not at all, I'm pleased she's happy, but I don't think Marie will be pleased to hear it," he said.

"Well, we can cross that bridge when we come to it," I said.

"I do love you," he said.

"I love you too," I replied.

"Marry me?" he said so suddenly, unexpectedly.

"What?" I exclaimed.

"Marry me," he repeated. "Let's do it here in Las Vegas at one of the little chapels down the strip. We can have a proper wedding when we get home but all the families here, let's do it now."

"Well, I've heard of spontaneous but this is something else," I said.

"Well," he said, holding both my hands.

"OK," I said, feeling absolutely overwhelmingly happy and surprised.

"Well, let's tell the family, I hope they are going to be as delighted as us," said Jack.

Within the next two days, everything was arranged. Chrissy and I had new dresses, a wedding dress for me that was short and very 60s in style which I felt would suit the venue as we had decided to be married in the Elvis Presley Chapel on the Strip and a bridesmaid dress for her that was way over the top with lace and frills but we let her have her choice. Her excitement knew no bounds but she did manage not to be sick at the ceremony.

Wills was best man and dad gave me away, he looked so proud I don't think he stopped smiling for a week. Jack presented me with the most beautiful heart-shaped diamond ring which matched the wedding rings we exchanged in the Chapple, which was terribly tacky but so enjoyable. It was so different from my first wedding but I enjoyed it a hundred times more.

Somehow the media people found out and they were waiting for us when we came out of the Chapple but for once no one seemed to mind we all allowed them to take as many photos as they wanted and we smiled and laughed and felt so happy that we all shared this special moment together. We had dinner at the Bellagio Hotel and I had never felt happier.

When we got home, it was to be greeted by a houseful of best wishes and gifts that were so unexpected. Jack immediately started to arrange a blessing in the little local church, followed by the biggest party I have ever been to. Life felt so good, Jack and I were so happy.

During these early days of Jack and I being together, I was working from home more and more when one day a call came through from Chrissy's school.

"Mrs London?" the voice asked. I still felt a little strange when someone called me this, but it was a nice feeling.

"Yes," I replied.

"Oh hello, this is Miss Jason, the Head Mistress from Christine's school."

"Hello," I said in reply. "Nice to speak to you. How can I help?"

"It's to let you know that Christine has sustained an injury whilst playing hockey and Matron thought that it seemed serious enough for her to go to A and E at the hospital. It is nothing too serious, we hope but we suspect she has a broken arm," said Miss Jason. "We thought that you and Mr London would like to be there for any treatment she may need."

"Yes, of course," I said. "Her father isn't here at the moment but I will inform him and arrange to meet him there at the hospital."

I left a message on Jack's phone, informed Edna and asked Charles to take me in the car to the hospital that Chrissy had been taken to.

On arrival I quickly found Matron and she said that Chrissy was currently in x-ray, having her arm x-rayed. I thanked her for her help but said she should get back to the school and that I would stay with Chrissy and await her father.

She handed over Chrissy's things, thanked me and left.

I sat in the relative's room and patiently waited for the doctor to update me about Chrissy. The waiting room was very typical of an A & E department, people rushing backwards and forwards, names being called and then unfortunates that were sat waiting to be seen. It seemed like an age and I was just thinking about going to the desk for an update when I heard my name spoken by someone standing nearby.

"Well, hello there," It was Ben's voice. "Of all the hospitals all over the world, you have to walk into mine," he said lyrically.

In all the rush, it had completely slipped my mind that I might walk into Ben here. We had rarely seen each other since the divorce. I tried to avoid places where I knew he would be if I could and it seemed a long time since I had seen him last. He looked very much as he always had, except a little older, more distinguished, if anything. I had heard that he was now a "Mr" rather than a "Dr". He kept in touch with my dad and dad often spoke of him and what he was doing, he said he always asked about me and if I was OK.

"What are you doing here?" he asked. "You're not hurt, are you?"

"No," I said. "It's Chrissy, she was hurt at school and I believe she's been taken to x-ray."

"Chrissy?" he enquired.

"Yes, Jack's daughter," I informed him.

"Oh," he said.

"I'll see what's happening if you like?"

"Thanks," I replied. "But I'm sure you have more important things to be doing."

"Not at all," he said. "I was about to take a break."

With that, he turned and left, only to return a few moments later. "She's still in x-ray. There's some delay, she will be a little while yet. I've told them to bleep me when she's on her way back. Coffee?"

"I'm not sure," I said. "Perhaps I should just wait."

"Nonsense, they will let me know," he said, taking my arm. "There's coffee ready made in my office."

With that, we walked along a small corridor until we reached Ben's office. There was a small anti room where his secretary was seated. She smiled at him as we walked by, the obvious adoration showing in her eyes.

"Just having coffee," he informed her. "Can you hold my calls for a while?"

He opened the door and ushered me inside, moving a pile of paperwork from a chair he indicated for me to sit down—He poured me a coffee exactly how I liked it and sat down at his desk.

It was then I noticed the photograph on his desk. I picked it up; it was of Jess and his two sons. They were all smiling, looking up at the camera. The boys were dressed in their school uniform which looked slightly big for them, it was obviously the day they started school and they must be a little older than that now. I put the photo back down, not making any comment.

"They're first day at school, they're older than that now, of course," Ben said.

I made no answer.

"I'd give it all up in a heartbeat to have you back, you know that, don't you?" he said quietly.

"What?" I replied, not quite believing I had heard him properly.

"I've never got over losing you," he said. "I couldn't believe my eyes when I saw you sat there. It was all my fantasies come true. I have often imagined running into you. You look exactly the same as you always did, except perhaps even more beautiful than I remember."

"Don't be ridiculous," I said. "Too much water has gone under the bridge; I'm married to Jack now."

"You can't love him, not like you loved me. We were so happy we had so much, the perfect couple, everyone said so surely you can remember how it felt I know I do."

"Yes, I remember how it felt but it seems a distant memory, like a dream I can't believe it really happened, so much time has gone by. My life is different now, I can't imagine life without Jack. I love him so much, he feels like the other half of me. I couldn't be any happier than I am now."

"No, you're lying I know you are. What we had can't be replaced. I know it can't. Losing you is something I don't think I will ever get over."

"You didn't lose me, Ben," I said quietly. "You threw me away without a second thought. How could I have meant so little to you for you to treat me that way?"

"I'm sorry," he said, getting up from the desk and coming over to stand beside me. He took my hand. "I would do anything to have you back, please say you feel the same."

"No, I don't," I said, getting up and turning to leave. "I feel nothing for you at all. You're something in the past that no longer has any impact in my life; I rarely ever think about you and when I do, they are not good feelings. I have the best lover I have ever had and nothing would ever convince me to leave him."

"Then what am I to you?" he asked.

"Nothing," I said. "Just someone I once knew. What is it the song says? Just a name on an old dance card."

I turned and left through the office door and going through the dimly lit outer office; I saw Jack standing in the light of the doorway and wondered how much he had heard. As I walked towards him, he nodded to the space just behind me beside the door to Ben's office and, as I slightly turned my head, I saw Jess standing in the shadows.

I saw the glistening of silent tears on her cheeks and knew that she had been stood there whilst listening to every word of the conversation Ben and I had just had I thought quite wickedly and not in the least guiltily that there was not a smirk on her face now. I turned and continued to walk towards Jack.

"Let's collect Chrissy and get out of here," I said, taking his hand.

He quickly pulled me towards him and kissed me hard. "Let's go," he said.

Chapter 12

Life became quieter. I was able to spend longer periods of time at home and although Jack toured a great deal, there were times I was able to go with him, although the experience soon started to pall.

For a start, Stephen was still employed by the band. Jack had been overruled by the other members about him being sacked. Neither of us wanted to share our reasons for not wanting him around so he stayed as road manager. He never missed the opportunity to have a snide remark at me but I took no notice as best I could, I ignored him. I still felt anxious seeing him around but I think he was more afraid of Jack than he was inclined to score points against me but I never really trusted him.

When touring, we visited so many exciting cities but were unable to find very little time to explore or get to know them. As soon as we arrived, we had to leave again and be on our way to the next venue. Jack was different when he was working, he was consumed with the performance. I always said he fed on the adoration.

That's why he remained so slender, adoration had no calories. He was a consummate professional entertainer, everything had to be just right and although he never showed it, I was definitely second best during these times a little bit of a spare part. So eventually I joined him less and less, preferring to spend time at home.

This was a new experience for me I had never been a home bod, always preferring to be at the forefront of business and helping to run a successful practice but I realised my health and energy was not what it used to be and I noticed how much I had been missing. I had never spent the time with my mother during her illness that I should have done and I wanted to be more a part of my father's life.

I did not want to look back and feel that I had missed out on a relationship with him. I enjoyed spending time with Chrissy too. We became firm friends and enjoyed each other's company. We shopped together, had lunch and enjoyed the theatre together, all the things a mother would do with a lovely daughter.

Wills spent as much time as he could at home, although university and his studying took up most of his time. He became more and more independent of the family but we were all so proud of him especially when he gained a first-class degree and secured a place at one of the most prestigious hospitals in London.

Although Chrissy was not as academic as Wills, she did well in her exams and decided to study art history at university and went into halls for the first year.

The house became quiet, although weekends often saw both Wills and Chrissy with various friends staying overnight. I enjoyed these times, life was good and I truly felt blessed.

The house needed very little maintenance and I turned my attention to the garden. I researched the history of the garden from local books and discovered at one time there was a knot garden just outside the sitting-room windows.

So, after some careful planning and taking instruction from a landscaping expert, I re-installed it. Jack liked it so much, although he knew very little about gardening, he asked me to pretty the front of the house as well. So I threw myself into this with renewed vigour and energy, it felt like I had escaped from my former life and I enjoyed the experience more than I imagined I could.

Amos's partner John recovered from cancer and went into remission, enabling both him and Amos to resume work. The clinics were now run completely by the Canadian group, although Amos and I both sat on the board of Directors. We went back to having a small private practice seeing a few private patients.

With some of the money we earned from that sale of the business, we discussed starting a foundation to help children with mental health problems and worked hard at setting this up. In the end, John Cutler and Jack decided they too wanted to be part of the foundation so it successfully went ahead.

John, Keith's son made a good recovery and he was so enthusiastic about helping others. Amos and I employed him in the foundation and he worked hard and after a little while became a very valued member of the team. He became engaged to one of our volunteers and his parents thanked me every time we met, although I told them John had achieved this but they still thanked me.

Keith decided to retire from the band due to increasing ill health issues and Jack and the management team auditioned several guitarists eventually deciding on a young man called Robin Lovejoy and he moved in with Jack and me for several months whilst he got to know the band and their music. He seemed to bring a new and invigorating jolt to the band and a new album was soon in production, with a tour being organised to promote it.

There was no sign of Jack ever slowing down or retiring; in fact, he seemed to be working harder than ever. Chrissy started to spend more weekends at home and it soon became obvious that there was a deep attraction developing between herself and Robin but as Jack and I both liked him we were happy that she was changing from being a very challenging teenager into a beautiful young woman.

After finishing his medical internship, Wills joined a well-known charity and started working all over the world wherever he was needed. Both of Jack's children had grown into well rounded, happy individuals and were a credit to us all.

Chapter 13

It always amazes me that when a traumatic event happens in your life, there is very often no inkling beforehand that your life is about to change so dramatically. You would think there would be some sort of indication that would give you a clue but I think it is better that we cannot see into the future. And so it was that warm summer day in June that our lives changed, perhaps forever.

I had awoken early and felt like getting up straight away, which was unusual for me. I was a night owl rather than a morning lark. The sun was streaming into the bedroom windows and the French lace that hung on either side made pretty patterns on the walls.

It's going to be a nice day, I thought as I looked around the room with its gold and white decorations. Jack had said he liked the way I had decorated my bedroom at my own home so he had wanted me to recreate the colour scheme here when I moved in and it worked. This room was obviously larger but I enjoyed altering it. Out went the heavy four-poster bed and I created a lighter, more modern look. It was not too feminine but it had an opulent look without it being OTT.

I had a fairly clear day so I decided to complete several chores that I had been putting off for some time. It was my God Daughter's birthday and although I had sent a card, I wanted to order some flowers to be delivered to her. Jack would be back in a couple of days and that would mean my time would not be my own. So I dressed casually in jeans and a plain white tee-shirt thinking to myself 'would there be a time when I would be too old for denim?' and after breakfast I went straight to my small study/sitting room to catch up on correspondence and phone calls to neglected friends and family.

The sun streamed into the room and that feel-good factor engulfed me. I opened the long windows and breathed in the scented air from the garden. I remember feeling how wonderful everything seemed sitting here in my pretty sitting room with its chintzy chair and sofa and the long pile carpet. The rest of the house had wide old oak floor boards which were quite dark.

When I first moved into this sprawling 17th century manor house, this room was originally the breakfast room but it had never been used and because the main sitting room was very masculine, consisting of huge brown leather sofas and a television screen big enough to be a cinema with every electronic gaming device you could think of. I asked Jack if I could make this small room that overlooked the garden into a feminine sitting room just for my own use. Jack did not mind he wanted me to feel at home.

Now this was the room everyone seemed to gravitate to and when Edna had her evening off, this is where we sat with supper trays on our laps. Jack was usually found here lounging on the small sofa with his legs dangling over the arm. I was glad people found it comfortable in here. The other room became more of a games room for the boys. That's where they relaxed and behaved like children again, except that the bar was always open and the beer flowed freely.

I was not long into my tasks when I noticed Edna, our housekeeper, standing in the doorway. "There are two policemen here to see you, madam."

"Really?" I answered. "You had better show them in." I wondered how many parking tickets Jack had forgotten to pay now.

"Good morning, Mrs London," the elder of the two said. "I am Detective Sergeant Groves and this is Detective Constable Evans." He briefly waved his warrant card at me. They both looked unmistakably like policemen although inevitably very young, but they say that's a sign of getting old, don't they?

"Please do come in and sit down. Can I offer you coffee? I was about to have some."

"Yes, thanks," said the elder of the two. I nodded to Edna and she disappeared.

"How can I help you?" I asked.

"Mrs London, can you confirm that you have a daughter by the name of Christine London?" said DS Groves. Suddenly I felt uneasy, the earlier feel-good factor disappeared and I was left with a feeling of foreboding. "Yes," I replied. "Well, actually, Chrissy is my stepdaughter. Why, has there been an accident, has something happened?"

"We are sorry to bear such bad news, but we have to inform you, Mrs London, that Christine was found dead at her home this morning." I felt as if I had been hit by a sharp blow in the pit of my stomach. My chest tightened and I could hardly catch my breath.

"I'm sorry, I don't understand," I gasped. "How, what happened? I only spoke to her yesterday, she was fine, was it some sort of accident?"

"It would appear," DS Groves said very quietly, "that she took her own life."

"No," I said. "It can't be. She was so happy yesterday, she said she had something wonderful to tell me."

My view shifted from DS Groves' face and I found myself looking at a small silver-framed photograph of a little girl at her ballet class. She was turned sideways on and the long black ringlets of her hair fell downwards against her bright chubby face. Her thick dark lashes framed eyes which were looking down at pointed toes encased in soft pink leather ballet pumps tied with pink ribbons around ankles finishing in bows above tiny heels. The one visible hand was holding her tutu.

I felt a gasp at the back of my throat, which sounded like a sob as I realised that this little girl was no more, a beautiful life gone forever. I could feel silent tears trickle down my cheeks.

"Madam, what is it? What's happened?" asked Edna, coming back into the room. The DC took the tray from her and placed it on the table. He then explained I had had a bit of a shock.

"It's Chrissy;" I said "She's been found dead."

"What? No, that can't be. Oh madam, no, how awful." Edna visibly went pale and her hand came up to her mouth. For the first time since I had known her, she sat down uninvited beside me.

"Before we precede any further, we will need someone to identify her, although we are fairly sure it is her, she was found in her flat. Is Mr London here? Could he do this?" asked DS Groves.

"No, he is out of the country on tour. Is it something I can do?" The DC had poured the coffee and was handing me a cup. My hand was shaking as I took it from him. "If you feel up to it, that would be very helpful," said DS Groves.

My mind suddenly seemed to be in a fog. I wiped my face with my hand. I needed to tell Jack, but how? I thought it was something I should do face to face. "Edna, I need to speak to Julie. Would you be good enough to get her on the phone?" I asked.

Edna still looked shocked, but she immediately got up. "Yes, of course," she said and left the room.

"DS Groves, I would like to tell my husband personally and to do that I need to get to Paris where the band is performing tonight. Will you be able to keep it from the press until I have done that? I don't want him to read it in the newspapers before I can speak to him."

"We can try," said DS Groves. "We can't release any details until we have a proper identification."

Edna returned with the phone. "Mr Jack's secretary is on the line for you, madam. I have explained the circumstances."

I took the phone from her; "Julie, I need a flight to Paris." I looked at DS Groves. "Midday?" The DS nodded. "And if you could arrange a car to meet me to take me to tonight's venue. It's urgent. If you cannot get me on a regular flight, try to hire a private plane. It's important I get there as soon as possible." I ended the call knowing that Julie would carry out the task efficiently. She was a good secretary and Jack's personal assistant.

"Can I follow you in my own car, DS Groves and then I will go directly to the airport?"

"Yes, Mrs London, we will wait outside for you." The two policemen got up and left.

"Edna, can you ask Charles to bring the car round and I will go pack the few things I need."

Edna followed the policemen out and I went upstairs. I don't remember what I put into my overnight bag but I remembered to grab my passport and my sunglasses hoping to hide my eyes so no one would see me crying or recognise me. I picked up a short black leather jacket but felt I did not have time to change and then dashed downstairs.

As I got into the waiting car, I could see by his face that Edna had told Charles the bad news. I remembered that, of course, they all had known the children longer than me so it must have been very upsetting for them all.

"Can you just follow the police car?" I asked Charles. "And then I will need to be taken to the airport."

My phone rang; Julie had managed to get me on the 2:30 p.m. flight to Paris. She would meet me at the airport with the all the travel documents. She said she would accompany me as she was sure she could be of use at this awful time. I thanked her and ended the call.

How was I going to tell him? His baby girl was dead. The apple of her father's eye, twenty-three years old and dead. I could not believe it; I wiped a tear away I can't break down now I have a task to perform, I said to myself. My stomach was churning and I felt physically sick.

The local mortuary was cold and I pulled my jacket tightly around me. No sunlight seemed to reach the windows while the walls, maybe because they were painted a stark white, made it feel so cold. I didn't even know this building was here and yet I must have passed it so many times. The young mortuary official was solicitous and offered his condolences. He was a tall gaunt looking young man and looked just how you would imagine a mortuary official should look.

I was shown into a room that looked a little like a small chapel. At the one end was a window with square coloured panes and there were unlit candles on a table covered with a purple cloth, I remember thinking "I wonder who decided that purple should be the colour of death."

My mind was wondering all over the place anything not to think about what was actually going on. The body was covered and lay in front of me. It looked tiny and I began to think that it could not possibly be Chrissy, but then the mortuary official removed the white sheet covering her face. I noticed how calm she looked as if she was just asleep. The vision of that little girl in her ballet dress came into my mind as I looked down at her.

"Can you confirm that this is your stepdaughter, Miss Christine London?" DS Groves asked.

"Yes," I said and that's when my legs buckled and everything went black.

When I came to, the mortuary official was waving some sort of a noxious substance under my nose and I was sitting on a chair outside the viewing room.

"I am so sorry," I said and the mortuary official said.

"It's OK, it's the shock." He moved away and the DC handed me a glass of water. I thanked him. I took a large gulp. "Are you feeling better now? Your colour is starting to come back," he said to me. I nodded and thanked him.

There were papers to sign but still before I knew it, I was back in the car and soon at the airport. Julie met me. She had picked up our tickets and had a coffee for me.

"I am so sorry," she said. I thanked her and took some of the hot coffee. I have booked myself to come with you as I am sure Jack and yourself will need things sorting out. She sat with me till we had to board. I think she spoke but I had no idea what she said, I was just aware of her holding my hand.

Julie and I settled into our seats and as I buckled my seat belt. I suddenly saw a small 12-year-old Chrissy sitting next to me.

"Mom, can you do my seat belt up for me," she said. It was the first time she had ever called me Mom. I wasn't quite sure I had heard her properly but after that moment that was what she called me. The first time Jack heard her say it, he hugged me and said now it feels like we are a real family. Tears started to roll down my cheeks and I think I cried for the whole time we were in the air.

The flight seemed to take forever. The car was waiting for us just as Julie had arranged but the traffic was awful. Of course, thousands of people were making their way to the venue and the performance had already started by the time we arrived.

I managed to find Izzy, the tour manager and told her I had some bad news for Jack when the performance had finished and she showed me to his dressing room. It was a small airless space and was way under the stage. I had waited in the same type of room many times, waiting for Jack to finish on stage. In the early days of our relationship, I had travelled with him as often as I could. He wanted me with him all the time. But the children's lives suffered so I stayed at home more and only visited on tour when the children could come too.

Izzy looked at me, concerned and I realised that the way I looked must have shown how dreadful the news must be. She left me in the dressing room and I noticed before the door closed that she and Julie were deep in conversation.

I sat listening to the muted music, trying to compose myself for the task ahead. I started to feel light-headed and realised I had not eaten since early this morning when the door opened and one of the many stage hands brought me a tray with sandwiches and coffee with a brandy. Izzy, I thought, how thoughtful of her.

I heard the set end and then the encore begin; it would not be long now. I started to tremble a little.

I heard laughter on the stairs and heard Jack's voice. He burst into the room laughing and saw me sitting there. "Darling, what a surprise. I am so pleased to see you." He took me in his arms and kissed me and then he looked into my eyes and he knew there was something wrong.

"What's the matter? What's happened?" he asked. "Are you ill?"

"No, I'm OK, I'm so sorry, it's Chrissy," My voice faltered.

"What is it?" he asked again, more urgently now.

I sat down and he sat next to me he was still holding onto me. "Chrissy was found dead this morning. They think she committed suicide."

"What? No, that's not right. She was fine I spoke to her yesterday. She was happy. You've made a mistake."

"I'm sorry. It's true. I had to identify her this morning." It was then that I started to cry, I couldn't hold back the tears any longer. I then realised that Robin, the bass guitarist, was stood in the open doorway. He must have heard everything I had said. He was the new younger member of the band and he and Chrissy had been in a relationship since the beginning of the year.

"I was going to ask her to marry me this weekend. I've even bought the ring," he said. The sadness suddenly seemed even worse.

I got up and went over to him. "I am so sorry," I said. It seemed inadequate. There seemed to be lots of questions from Jack and Robin and I tried to answer as many as I could but I was feeling weak and so overwhelmed. There was a knock on the door and Izzy came in.

"I have taken the decision to cancel the last two days of the tour. I will take care of everything, the notifications and the promotors, everything. You don't have to worry," she said. "There is a plane ready to take you back to the UK tonight. Julie and I will deal with everything else."

The rest of the band joined us. They all seemed so quiet as if they did not know what to say. As we left, I noticed the noise in the auditorium had dissipated and there was an eerie silence everywhere. Soon the clean-up teams would arrive and sweep away all the rubbish, make everything clean and new again. I wish they could do that for us. Put everything back the way it was when the day had begun. In the space of a few hours, everything had changed, nothing would ever be the same again.

Chapter 14

I slept all the next day. It had been about 6.30 a.m. when we arrived home, we were all exhausted. Robin came with us, he did not want to be by himself and I was glad we could all be together. I awoke alone in bed; I did not know where Jack was. I had been aware of him coming and going the previous day but I had been too wiped out to do anything more than sleep. Edna entered the room with a tray as soon as I opened my eyes. I don't know how she knew but she always seemed to be aware of my waking.

"I've bought you a light breakfast, madam. You ate nothing yesterday and you must be hungry."

"Thank you, Edna, it's so kind of you. Do you know where Mr Jack is?"

"He's out walking the dogs. He and Mr Robin were up early. They ate and were gone quite soon after that."

After eating, I showered and dressed, suddenly wanting to feel quite human again.

Coming down stairs I heard Jack's voice, he sounded quite annoyed and I realised he was on the phone in the study. As soon as I entered, I could tell by his face and stance he was speaking to Marie, his ex-wife and the children's mother. She had abandoned the children when her marriage to Jack was over. Leaving them in his care, she took off with the latest young man in her life and never really ever looked back.

The divorce bought her wealth she had never had before and there had been no stopping her from living a life with one man after another. Jack had always described her as a sex addict she just couldn't stop. Her infidelities during their marriage had been legendary. She rarely saw the children whilst they grew up and they had less and less contact with her.

"You know that is just so typical of you," I heard him say. "It's all about how it affects you, regardless of anyone else."

"No, you bloody can't come and stay here," Jack said, seeming to be getting angrier and angrier.

"You know what? Do what you bloody well want to. I just don't care."

The phone was slammed down rather abruptly.

"She says she has not got a suitable black dress to wear," he said, trembling. "Can you believe it? I inform her that her daughter is dead and she is wondering what she has to wear."

"I don't know why you still get upset about her. You know she does not feel things the way everyone else does. Did she expect to come and stay here with us?"

"Yes, this is where the media will be focussed so this is where she will want to be, along with that awful Argentine gigolo. Do you know I think she is about to marry him?"

He was quiet for a moment but he soon regained his composure. It was not very often he lost his temper, but Marie certainly knew which buttons to press, but then again she had installed most of them.

"I still have not managed to get in touch with Wills. I don't want him reading about it in the press before I can speak to him. I have left several messages but still haven't been able to reach him."

"He may be out of reach. Do you think he will be able to get home?" I asked.

"I don't know. I would like to see him, but flights from the place in Zimbabwe are not easy to be had. It may take a few days to extricate him from the charity too, especially if he is the only doctor available."

He pulled me close to him and buried his head in my shoulder. We stood like that for several minutes until we heard voices in the hall.

It was Edna and Robin.

"There are a few members of the press at the gates, Mr Jack. Would you like me to ask Charles to move them away?" she asked.

"No, just leave them be. They will soon get tired and move away. Do you think we could have some coffee?"

"Yes, of course. I'll deal with it right away," she said, already halfway down the hall.

"Morning, Robin," I said as he moved towards me and kissed me on the cheek.

"Are you feeling better after your sleep?" he asked.

"I think it was more of a comma than a sleep. I was absolutely exhausted. The shock just knocked me sideways," I said.

"Thanks for letting me stay. I just did not want to be on my own. At least here she still seems to be around somehow."

We moved into the sitting room and the coffee appeared almost immediately. We all sat there not saying anything when the phone rang. I answered it and was pleased to hear Wills' voice on the other end.

"Hold on, Wills, I will get your father to speak to you," I said.

"It's Wills," I said and handed him the phone.

It was a difficult conversation. How do you explain to someone their little sister was dead? They spoke for some time and when the call was over Jack said, "He says he'll be on the next available flight."

"I'm so glad," I said. "I think we all need to be together."

The day wore on slowly. The phone calls from friends and family started to come through as the news leaked out and also calls from the press. How did they find out our private numbers?

None of us wanted to speak to anyone and to keep repeating the same thing over and over again was purgatory. Eventually we asked Julie, Jack's p.a. to come over and start fielding the calls. She soon arrived and started to handle everything so efficiently. We were so grateful to her.

By late afternoon, I started to feel stifled and felt the need to get out into the fresh air. Jack and I decided to go for a walk. We were quite lucky, in that we could walk for quite a while without coming across prying eyes. We set off across the fields with the dogs running about our legs. It felt good to be outside.

We entered the woods on the north side of the property. We could not see the house from here so we felt completely alone, which was rare as there always seemed to be someone close by. I loved these woods; there was an air of quiet and peace it felt so good to be with Jack just by ourselves. The sun was shining and it felt unreal that the world was just carrying on as normal. I started to believe it had all been a dream and that Chrissy was still alive and happy with her whole life before her.

"What did she say to you that last time she spoke to you?" Jack suddenly asked, breaking my thoughts.

"She was happy, she was looking forward to the tour ending so she could be with Robin. She said she missed him so and she had some secret news for us all. Why would she suddenly feel nothing was worth living for? Something terribly must have happened after we spoke, although I can't imagine what. I have gone over and over that last conversation. If something had upset her, she would have spoken to me. You know, she always confided in me."

"Yes, I know," he said. "She would speak to you before me very often. I just am so lost. What could have made her do this?"

We walked on in silence, each with our own thoughts. Both at such a loss to understand.

Chapter 15

When we approached the house returning from our walk, I noticed a car parked outside the entrance with two men beside it.

"I hope they haven't let anyone in," said Jack. "I really don't think I can face anyone just now."

As we got closer, I could see that one of the men was DS Groves, although I did not recognise the second man.

"It's the police," I said to Jack. "They said they would be back to see us within the next few days."

When we were close enough, I held out my hand to DS Groves and said, "This is my husband, Jack. Jack, this is DS Groves that came to inform me about Chrissy."

"Hello," DS Groves said. "This is Detective Inspector Somerset."

We both shook hands with the Inspector.

"We need to speak to you both and give you an update now that a post-mortem has been carried out," said DI Somerset. "Is this something that can be done now?"

"Yes, of course," said Jack. "Please come this way."

We removed our coats and outside shoes and showed both men into the sitting room.

"Please," I said, offering them both a seat.

"Thank you, Edna," I said as Enda placed a tray on the side table. I poured tea for Jack and our two guests.

They both thanked me and DS Groves took out a small pocketbook.

"It has become clear from the post mortem that has been carried out," he started to say.

Jack took my hand. I had a feeling he was thinking about Chrissy and how upsetting to treat her in that way.

"That your daughter, Miss Christine London, did not, in fact, commit suicide," DS Groves continued.

"Are you saying it was an accident, after all?" asked Jack.

"No, we believe that Christine was killed and then it was covered up to make it look like suicide," said DS Groves.

"Oh my god," I said. "Can this possibly get any worse?"

"How was she killed?" asked Jack.

"We believe she was hit on the head or fell hitting her head on a hard object and we believe from her injuries that she fought her killer very hard before she died. Her death was then made to look like suicide."

"Do you have any idea who it was?" asked Jack.

"No, not at the moment," replied DI Somerset. "But we do have DNA and a full forensic team is now at her flat. They will find something, believe me, when I say no one cleans up as well as they think they do."

"We want to ask you if you know of anyone who could do this. Did she have any enemies or had she received any threats of any kind? Anything that you could tell us about her life would help us," he continued.

"No," Jack said, looking at me. "I don't know anyone who would wish her harm. She had a lot of friends but there was no animosity between them, not that I know of."

"She was well liked," I said. "She was about to become engaged to Robin, one of the members of the band. The last time I spoke to her she was really happy she could not contain herself that's why when we heard she had committed suicide we found it so hard to believe. In fact, she told me she had some wonderful secret news to tell us."

"Do you know what that news was?"

"No, she said she wanted to tell Robin first and then Jack and myself."

I saw DI Somerset look at DS Groves and he nodded his head.

"We will give you some information which you should be aware of as it will be reported at the inquest," said DS Groves, lowering the sound of his voice. "Your daughter was 12 weeks pregnant. Do you think that was the news she was so happy about?"

I stifled a sob and Jack grabbed my hand.

"Yes," said Jack. "She would have been overjoyed by being pregnant and it would have been something she would have wanted to tell Robin first."

"I am sorry," said DI Somerset. "I can only imagine how hard all this must be for you."

I excused myself. I knew I was about to burst into tears and I did not want to do that in front of anyone. I went upstairs and into our bedroom by then I was sobbing uncontrollably. A daughter and a potential grandchild, I thought to myself. How could anyone be so cruel?

After a little while, I heard the policemen leave and Jack came up the stairs.

"Are you OK? I have bought you a brandy. I think you most probably need it."

I thanked him through the sobs. I knew how he hated to see me cry but I just could not stop.

"I think I need to speak to Robin," Jack said. "He deserves to know first and then I will try to speak to Marie and then Will before we tell anyone else."

All I could do was nod my head. I was glad they were conversations I did not have to have.

I stayed in the bedroom till the sobs subsided and I had regained some composure. I then washed my face, replaced my makeup and went downstairs.

Jack was by himself and on entering, he poured me another drink. I noticed he had a drink in his hand too. I had not seen him drink since Christmas but I could fully understand his need now.

"How did Robin take it?" I asked.

"Not good. I think he's about to come apart at the seams."

"We must keep him here; we all need to support each other."

"I'm so glad I have you," he said.

Chapter 16

The next few weeks were purgatory. I could not believe the sun still rose every morning, just the same, as if nothing had changed. How could the world remain the same?

Jack walked around as if in a fog. He didn't eat or sleep but seemed to be drinking more than ever I remember him drinking since I had known him. He didn't want to talk and eventually just locked himself away in the studio; I felt so helpless.

"I don't know what to do, Amos," I said one day when Amos phoned to see how we were coping.

"Just be there for him," he answered. "Deal with everything that needs to be sorted out, the things he is just not facing that will help you too. It will give you something to focus on, keep you busy."

"Thank you, Amos," I said.

And that's what I did. I started with the funeral. The body had not been released yet but I started planning the church service and burial. I chose burial, although it was something that had never been discussed with Chrissy. Why would it have been? I broached the subject with Robin and although I could see it was painful for him to think about; he agreed with me that a burial seemed better than a cremation. I asked him to think about some music that she liked and he went away and sorted this out. I hope it helped him a little too.

The next painful experience was the inquest. I had never been to one before but sat listening to every detail of Chrissy's last moments of life spoken about so clinically without any emotion it was unreal as if it wasn't her at all just someone we vaguely knew. It hurt so much to know that her last moments on this earth were spent in terror and agony, that her friends and family were so totally unable to help her.

Jack looked awful, a shadow of his former self. He didn't carry any weight anyway but now he looked gaunt and frail I was really starting to worry about him.

The coroner's verdict was unlawful killing and with the police's OK the body was released.

When we got home, Jack disappeared straight away to the studio without any comment. This was not good so I decided to face him head on.

For the first time since we had been together, we had a terrible argument. We physically fought and in the end, he broke down completely sobbing uncontrollable clinging to me saying he thought it was his fault that he had done nothing to save her.

"What could you have done?" I asked him.

"I was her father, I was supposed to take care of her," he sobbed. "She was my daughter. I loved her so I should have been with her more let her know how much she meant to me."

"She knew how much you loved her and she loved you too," I said, holding him to me as tight as I could. "She thought you were the best dad in the world. She said to me she used to feel sorry for her friends that they didn't have you as a dad."

"That's the sort of thing she would say, always aware of other people."

"Yes, she always seemed aware of how lucky she was and how good her life was," I said. "But it didn't make her smug or unfeeling and I know she would not want to see you feeling like this."

"I know I'm being selfish wallowing in this self-pity it just hurts so much, it's a physical pain I feel and it won't go away."

"We will help each other," I said. "Let's start now this very second. Do something positive for Chrissy."

"What can I do for her now?" he said, sitting up and looking straight at me. "It's too late, there's nothing."

"You're wrong," I replied. "We can arrange her funeral and lay her to rest. Give her the peace she deserves, not leave her there in that cold place by herself."

He stopped crying and, as if a realisation came to him, said, "You're right, of course. I'm just thinking of myself, not her." He kissed my forehead, his face still wet from tears. "I think I would like to see her one last time to say goodbye. Can we do that?"

"Yes, of course, we can," I replied.

With that, he took my hand and we walked back to the house.

Chapter 17

The funeral was held at the little church in the town where our marriage was blessed and that's where Chrissy was buried. She had always had a thing about Angels watching over us, so Jack chose a stone Angel for her grave.

We asked for close friends and family only at the service but there were hundreds of people outside the church all trying to get a glimpse of Jack and members of the band that were in attendance.

The day was warm and the sun shone, which somehow helped us to get through the day. I think when someone dies, you don't start to get closure until the funeral is over and that's how it felt to me.

The day passed so slowly as if it was a dream sequence, not reality. The service was beautiful. Everyone seemed so distressed. Jack, myself, Robin and Wills clung to each other throughout the service and I felt sorry for Marie as she seemed to be on the side of the event that was happening. She came back to the house after the service with her young fiancée.

Later in the afternoon I found her sat on Chrissy's bed silently weeping.

"Are you OK, Marie? Can I get you anything?" I asked.

"No, thank you," she replied. "I can't believe I'll never see her again."

"I know she leaves a gaping hole in all our lives."

"You were so good to her, she liked you so much. She said you were like the big sister she always wanted. I know you were close and were here for her when I wasn't."

"You were her mom and she loved you."

"Thank you for that. You're very kind."

"If there is anything here of hers that you would like to have, please help yourself."

"The only thing is this photograph of the four of us on holiday in Spain in the early days before Jack's career took off. We were so happy, just an ordinary family like everyone else. I would like that if it's OK."

"Of course, whatever you would like," I said and quietly left her to her thoughts and let her get herself together.

When everyone had left and we had the house to ourselves, we sat down, exhausted. Robin told us he had decided he would be leaving the following day with Wills. The charity Wills was working for were building a hospital and they needed volunteers to help so Robin was going to go with Wills and try to do something where he could concentrate his mind on something else besides his loss and I felt it would be good for both him and Wills to have each other for a while.

Jack and I decided to close up the house and go away for a few weeks, try to recuperate and just be alone together. We both needed this and although Jack had been a little better since our talk, he still wasn't back to his old self. It would give him a chance to relax and focus on getting back to some sense of normality.

The police kept us updated with their investigation but there were no real suspects. They had DNA evidence and some CCTV footage of people coming and leaving Chrissy's building but as they informed us; it was still early days.

So we left for a private villa on Antigua, gave Edna and Charles time off, which they needed as much as any of us and we all tried to heal or at least recover well enough to cope with the future and the emptiness Chrissy's death had left in our lives.

The villa was lovely, it even had a recording studio but Jack wasn't interested. We sat by the pool, swam a little and held each other.

A friend invited us to join him and his wife on their yacht for a few days, which we decided to do and Jack was surprised to know I sailed and was able to handle the boat although I was a little rusty but soon got back into sailing. I had forgotten how much I loved sailing; it was invigorating and I had to work very hard to stop Jack from buying a boat as soon as we were back on dry land.

The following Sunday, the same friends took us up to Shirley Heights. Jack was suddenly at his ease. Everyone wanted to shake his hand, the rum flowed, the food cooked on open fires and the bands all wanted Jack to sit and listen to their music. The air was thick with whatever everyone was smoking and whether it was that or just the overall atmosphere we both felt euphoric and good for the first time in months.

The next day when I woke, Jack was already in the studio working. I didn't mind; it was good to see him interested in something. I didn't bother him. I just took my book and sat by the pool. It was evening when he emerged and was ravenous. We ate and he talked practically nonstop about the work he had been doing.

After a few days, he said there was enough work for an album and before I knew the band's manager and the band were in the villa with us and an album was put together. The main song which they chose for release as a single was called *Baby Girl* and it had a sort of reggae beat to it. It was very emotive and after hearing it just once, you seemed like you couldn't get the words and music out of your head.

It turned out to be the best-selling single of that year and the album went platinum within three weeks of being released. Everywhere we went, we heard the song playing and it felt that it had been Chrissy that had inspired her dad to write and compose the music.

When we arrived back in the UK, we decided to call the foundation we had set up as 'Chrissy's Foundation' and in some way it felt she would always be remembered as the kind, loving girl she was.

Chapter 18

Jack was away on the last leg of a far eastern tour with the last few dates in Europe but would be back by the end of the week, so like all the other times he was due home after a long time away from each other I had cleared my diary for a couple of weeks so we could spend some time together just being a couple again. Jack always came back totally exhausted and for the first few days it took him a while just to recuperate, to get back his strength and settle back into a normal routine.

He found it difficult to sleep at night, part of the jet lag, I suppose. Travelling from one country to another on a continuous basis put his body clock at odds with normal hours although the last leg of this current tour had been Europe so I hoped it wouldn't be as bad as if he was returning from the Far East or America.

I had missed him, although I had flown out to be with him a few days in Germany and we had a weekend together I was glad he was coming home. He was promising to go on these long tours less and less as he said he was getting tired easier and it was becoming harder to do continuous concerts. He would always want to perform, he loved it but felt that they would be more one offs rather that a run of 10 or 12 weeks.

I sensed immediately as I walked in the kitchen that something was wrong, both Charles and Edna jumped as I said good morning. They had been huddled together across the island unit looking at the newspaper. They looked up together, surprised to see me standing there. Edna quickly closed the paper.

"Good morning, madam," she said. "The coffee is fresh; shall I pour you a cup?"

"That would be lovely," I replied. "Something interesting in the paper?"

Edna looked at Charles quite nervously. Both hesitated a moment, then Charles picked up the paper and handed it to me.

I sat down at the breakfast table sipping my coffee, puzzled at his reaction. I did not have to open the paper, as the pictures were all over the front page. The headline was 'Jack the lad' and the pictures showed Jack in bed with a long dark-haired woman. The pictures showed a hotel bedroom with two people engaged in sex.

The women had her back to the camera but was shown straddling Jack with him laid on his back looking up at her. There were several other pictures of the two of them in different poses. I suddenly felt sick and rushed to the downstairs cloakroom. I just managed to reach the toilet before I was so violently sick. I collapsed to the floor.

How could he? Two nights ago when we spoke on the phone, he told me how he loved me and was so desperate to see me again and now this. Was it an affair or just a one-night stand? What did it matter? He had still cheated. Oh my God, how it hurt.

"Madam, are you OK?" Edna asked, standing in the doorway. "Let me help you up."

I had a job standing, my legs felt like jelly, my heart was thumping in my chest and my head ached.

"Come sit here and I'll fetch you a glass of water," said Edna, helping me back to the kitchen. "I'm so sorry, madam, I thought of hiding the paper but well, you would have seen it, eventually."

"Thank you, Edna," I said, gulping the water. "Well, I didn't expect that this morning. I don't know about my head in the toilet, my whole life seems to be heading that way."

"Oh no, madam, it must be some sort of mistake. I know Mr Jack loves you I've never seen him look at any other woman since that first night he brought you here. I knew even then that you were the one for him, it has to be some sort of mistake."

"Oh yes, it's a mistake alright and it's all of his making."

It took me a while before I was able to stand and leave the room. Edna wanted to make me breakfast but just the thought of food brought the nauseous feeling back. I went upstairs, splashed my face with cold water and lay on the bed until I could stop shaking and when I did, the images came back into my mind and I burst into tears, sobbing and was unable to stop.

I cried for a long time until there were no more tears, my eyes were red and sore, so I got up from the bed and splashed my face again putting some fresh makeup on but looking in the mirror I noticed how dreadful I looked.

"Can I get you anything, madam?" Edna asked, coming into the room. "Some tea perhaps?"

"Yes, thank you, Edna, that would be nice."

I took a deep breath. I needed to think. Should I pick up the phone and speak to him, ask him what the bloody hell he was playing at, but a slanging match over the phone wasn't the answer. Besides, he would only have to say he was sorry and tell me he loved me and I would forgive him, I loved him so I would forgive him practically anything.

I had to get away and think. Somewhere he couldn't reach me so to give me time. I am sure the papers would soon be hunting me as well. That's what I would do, get far away and think about how I wanted to deal with this.

Chapter 19

I answered three phone calls that day in the car on the way to the airport. The first one was from Amos.

"What's going on?" he asked. "I've just seen the papers, I can't believe it. Where are you? I phoned the house and they said you had left and they didn't know where you were going."

"I don't know where I'm going either," I said. "I'm just going to catch the first flight out and give myself time to think. Somewhere he can't find me."

"In other words you're running away again. Don't you think you should stay and sort it out with him?"

"No, I can't do that," I said. "He would only have to say he was sorry, look into my eyes and hold me. I would forgive him anything. You know how I feel about him."

"I also know how he feels about you. He loves you why would he do this?"

"Well, you can't dispute the evidence. It's there in black and white," I answered.

"Do you want to come and stay with us?" Amos asked. "You're always welcome, you know you are."

"Thanks," I said. "But it's the first place he would look for me."

"Are you sure?"

"Yes, I'll let you know where I am when I get there. Can you take care of work? I won't be away for long. I just need time to think."

The second call was from dad. He was really concerned for me but I didn't want to worry him so I just said I would call him later but not to worry about me I would be fine.

The third call was from Elaine, the wife of Keith, the original bass player in the band. She had also seen the papers and was concerned.

I explained what I was doing and she asked me not to leave.

"I have to get away, so I can think with a clear head. Somewhere Jack can't find me," I said.

"Look, don't leave the country, that's just too disruptive to your work and your friends and family would worry so much about you," she said. "We have a house in South Gloucestershire that we rarely use. There's a housekeeper that takes care of the place, she will look after you but give you space. Jack won't think of looking for you there. If you need to continue to go to work, it's not too much of a commute. It would be ideal."

"Are you sure?" I asked. "You won't tell him where I am, will you?"

"I don't suppose he will even think of asking us," she said. "I'll text you the address and speak to Julie, the housekeeper. Tell her to expect you. She's completely trustworthy and her discretion can be relied upon."

"Thank you, Elaine; it's very kind of you, I'm so grateful."

The next thing I did was visit Charles' friend, Jason Allan, the private detective. His office was not far from the airport. He was a tall, muscular, grey-haired man who, despite his age, was very youthfully good looking. He spoke quietly and listened attentively to everything I said. He knew who I was and had seen the photographs of Jack in the papers.

"As you can see from these," I said, pointing the pictures out in the copy I had brought with me. "There must have been someone else in the room with a camera, which makes me very suspicious because whatever Jack is, he is not an exhibitionist."

"So," said Mr Allan. "What is it you want me to do?"

"Firstly," I replied. "I want you to find out who this woman is. The paper just describes her as an unknown woman, I want to know if this was a one-night stand or has Jack been seeing her for some time. Knowing who she is will help me determine that. Secondly, who gave the photos to the newspapers? Was it a setup? This does not mean I don't think Jack would do something like this. In fact, at the moment, I don't know what to think. I'm so upset."

"I can imagine," he said. "I do understand I'll do everything I can to help."

"Thank you," I said, suddenly feeling a little bit back in control and doing something positive about the situation.

I told him I would contact him with a telephone number where I could be reached but left him with my mobile if he needed more information.

He said he would be in touch as soon as he had any information and we shook hands and I left.

Charles asked if Jason had been able to help.

"Yes, he was very understanding," I said. "Thank you. Charles, can I ask you to keep this visit between ourselves for the moment? I know your loyalty lies with Jack but until Mr Allan has any information, I would rather not let Jack know."

I still got Charles to drop me at the airport. I wanted everyone to believe I was out of the country. As soon as the car was well out of the way, I got into a taxi and gave the address of Keith and Elaine's house, arriving late in the afternoon. The taxi driver went away with the best fare of the day and I entered the house that was to be my home for the next few weeks.

Julie, the housekeeper, was very welcoming. There was a pot of coffee waiting for me as soon as I arrived and Julie took my bags up to my room whilst I drank it and even unpacked for me.

The house was a large manor house made from Cotswold stone and sat on extensive grounds outside a small village. It was completely private and Julie said it would be unlikely that I would run into anyone who may know or recognise me.

The next few days I spent lazily being waited up on; I think Julie enjoyed the company and the opportunity to be busy. She explained that Keith and Elaine rarely used the property now that their children were grown up and there had been some recent discussions about selling up. I asked Julie what she would do then and she said she would look for something else, good housekeepers were always in demand and I replied I could understand that.

Julie was a good-looking shapely blond in about her mid-forties. She was extremely efficient and would have been an asset to anyone. She was also a Cordon Bleu cook so I decided to make use of the gym in the basement to counteract the beautiful food I was being served three times a day.

I caught up on correspondence and telephones calls, walked in the grounds and slept surprisingly very soundly, anything rather than think about my love life. That's if I still had a love life. Jack had been on tour for almost three months and I had seen very little of him during that time, although he continued to phone every day. Had he been seeing someone else during that time? I don't know I hoped not, but I really did not know.

By the end of the week, he was back in the country and from telephone calls from all and sundry; he was going crazy looking for me. Amos said he was calling personally into the clinics every day and in the end Amos had needed to be quite strong telling him to keep away as his behaviour was becoming disruptive. Dad was also being bombarded with calls and visits and in the end, I decided to speak to Jack. I couldn't do this face to face so when he phoned my mobile one day, I picked up his call.

"Hello," he said quite normally. "Where are you? I need to speak to you. Please let me see you."

"No Jack," I replied. "I need some time away from you; I need time to think about us and how much you have hurt me."

"I'm so sorry," he said. "I've never wanted to hurt you please believe me."

"Do you love her?" I asked.

"Good god no," he exclaimed. "I don't even know who she is. Please believe me."

I felt a little relieved, although I had started to shake and become tearful.

"I need some time. Please give me that and stop harassing everyone we know to find out where I am. When I'm ready, I will speak to you. In the meantime, please leave me alone and stop trying to contact me."

"If that's what you want but I think we need to talk about this," he said.

"I know," I said. "But not yet." And at that, I ended the call.

As far as I know, he did stop trying to get in touch but I knew it would not last long and I had to reconcile with myself that I needed to make a decision about the future.

I decided to go back to work and start seeing my patients. Perhaps sorting out other people's problems would help me sort out my own. So I went back to work. At first there were some strange looks from people I came across and quite a lot of conversations that finished as soon as I walked into a room but eventually people found something else to discuss and my day-to-day life went back to normal except I did not go home at night to my husband but went on avoiding the confrontation that was inevitable.

Amos was solicitous as usual I'm sure he worried about me and kept telling me to sort things out but, unlike his patients, I ignored all the good advice he gave me.

We needed to work on the setup of 'Chrissy's Foundation' and I now concentrated on this as another diversion from dealing with my personal life.

After two weeks throwing myself into my work, Amos came into my office. Closing the door behind him, he pulled a chair around to my side of the desk and sat down.

"We need to resolve this situation between you and Jack I can't allow you to keep burying your head in the sand. You're not eating, you look ill because I bet you're not sleeping, you're unhappy everyone can see that and your patients can see it too," he said quite forcibly. "Pick up the phone, speak to Jack and make arrangements to meet him and talk."

I hung my head and felt ashamed of myself.

"You're right, of course. I just couldn't face things head on," I admitted.

He picked up the phone from the desk and handed me the receiver.

"I'm not leaving here until you speak to him," Amos said, pushing the receiver to my face and I knew he meant it.

I took the receiver from him and dialled Jack's number and he picked it up almost before it had started to ring.

"Hello," I said so casually. I saw Amos leave the room.

"Hello my love, it's so good to hear your voice," he said.

"I think I'm ready to meet and talk," I said with a faltering voice.

"Anywhere, anytime," came the reply.

"I'm in London for the next few days; would you like to meet at the flat for dinner tomorrow?" I asked.

"Yes, of course. What time?"

"Shall we say seven?"

"Thank you. I look forward to it," he answered, sounding brighter.

I put the phone down and immediately started to feel dread. When I got back to South Gloucester that night, I told Julie I would be staying in London the following night and informed her I had plucked up the courage to meet with Jack.

"I'm so pleased," she said. "I was beginning to think it was never going to get sorted.

"He's coming to the flat for dinner although I will be in such a tis about meeting him I'm sure I won't be able to cook anything edible."

"I'll tell you what we could do," she said. "I could do with a few days in London myself. Why don't I come with you, cook your dinner and then disappear? That will give you time to pretty yourself up, go and get a pampering or something and feel good when you meet him."

"That's a marvellous idea and a great plan," I said. "You can stay at the flat; it's got separate quarters you can use. Oh thank you Julie, you're a godsend."

So we drove into London together the following day and I went into the clinic with Julie going off shopping. We arranged to meet back at the clinic at 4:00

p.m. and sure enough, at 3:55, I had a call from reception to say my visitor had arrived. I was with Amos when I took the call and suggested he come down and meet my new saviour.

"Hello Julie," I said as we met at reception. This is my colleague Amos. I'm sure you have heard me speak of him."

"Yes, of course," she said, holding out her hand and smiling at him.

"It's nice to meet you Julie; I've heard a lot of good things about you."

At that moment, Julie's phone started to ring.

"Oh, I need to get this," she said.

"That's OK I'll take the shopping and meet you downstairs in the car park," I said, picking up Julie's bags.

"Bye," said Amos. "I wish you all the best for tonight," he said, kissing me on the cheek.

I entered the lift and pressed the button for the basement car park. The lift doors opened and I alighted and, whilst walking to the car, fumbled in my bag for my car keys.

"Mrs London," I heard a voice call and turning to see who it was, I suddenly felt a sharp pain on the side of my head and I felt as if a dark curtain had enveloped me as I fell to the floor.

"You bloody fool, I think you've killed her." I heard a voice say as the darkness came.

Chapter 20

When I opened my eyes, I seemed to be in a grey fog. I could not focus my eyes but eventually I realised that the room was lit very dimly. My head hurt, I mean really hurt and my throat was so dry I was unable to speak. I was aware of someone holding my hand rather too tightly but I was unable to move my hand away. I heard a voice; it sounded like Amos and for a while I could not think why he should be in my bedroom. Is it my bedroom? I don't think it is. Where am I? I started to move but the pain in my head stopped me.

"She's awake," I heard Amos say. "I'll get the doctor."

The doctor, I thought, why does he need a doctor?

"Oh my God, you're awake." It was Jack's voice. I realised he was the one holding my hand. He leaned over me and kissed my forehead. "You have had us all so worried."

I tried to speak but I just made a croaking noise.

"Are you alright?" Jack asked. "Can I get you a drink?"

"Mm," I managed to croak.

He placed a straw in my mouth and I sipped some cool water. It felt wonderful.

"So you're back with the living, Mrs London," said a young man who came into the room with a nurse and Amos. "How do you feel?"

"My head hurts," I managed to reply.

"I'm not surprised, the knock you took," said the doctor. "We are all amazed it's still attached to your body."

Jack was still gripping my hand, which felt strange for some reason but I couldn't figure out why. My head hurt too much to ask myself questions. I couldn't figure out what was going on.

"If you gentlemen would leave us alone for a few minutes whilst we check Mrs London over," said the nurse.

Jack leaned over and kissed me again, finally letting go of my hand, smiling and left with Amos.

"You most probably have a hundred questions and are feeling very confused," said the doctor. "But just give yourself a little time and relax. Everything will come back to you. Don't push yourself. OK?"

"OK," I replied.

He checked me over and the nurse made some notes on the records she was holding.

"Well, everything seems fine. You're doing well," said the doctor.

"I'm going to ask your husband and friend to give you some time to rest for a while. It will let you relax without you wanting to ask them questions, which you will do if they both come back in," he said. "Is there anything I can get for you?"

"I'm terribly thirsty," I said.

He nodded to the nurse and she passed me some more water, which I gulped at.

"Now Nurse Robbins is just outside the door," said the doctor. "So if you want anything, just press the buzzer. In the meantime, try to relax."

The next time I woke, sunlight was streaming through the windows and the room looked very different. Nurse Robbins was beside the bed, holding my wrist.

"Well, good morning, sleeping beauty," she said. "I was beginning to wonder if you were ever going to wake up."

"How long have I been asleep?" I asked.

"About fourteen hours, but don't worry, it's good for your recovery. Now, how about some breakfast?" she asked.

"Yes, that would be lovely, especially if it includes coffee," I replied.

"I'll see what I can do. Are you up to visitors?" she asked. "Your husband and friend are outside."

"Yes, of course," I said but for some reason I felt a reluctance inside which I couldn't explain.

Before she left, she adjusted the bed and rearranged the pillow so I was sitting up. I suddenly realised that although my head still hurt, it was a hundred times better than the day before.

Jack came through the door first and was beside me before I could blink.

"Whoa, you look so much better this morning," he said. "How are you feeling?"

"A lot better, thanks," I replied. "My head still hurts but not as bad as yesterday."

He kissed my cheek and grabbed my hand, bringing it to his lips and kissing my fingers.

Amos came towards me and kissed my cheek.

"You certainly have some colour in your face again," he said. "I don't think I have ever seen anyone look so pale, your skin was almost translucent."

"Everyone was so worried about you, you gave us such a scare," said Jack.

Nurse Robbins came in with a tray.

"Here you are," she said. "Scrambled egg, toast, orange juice and hot coffee."

"That sounds wonderful," I replied. "I can't understand it but I am so hungry suddenly."

"There are two police offices outside who need to speak to you when you are ready," said Nurse Robbins.

"Police offices?" I asked whilst sipping the hot coffee, which tasted wonderful. "Why should they need to speak to me?"

"It's about the attack. They want to ask you what happened," said Amos.

"What attack?" I asked, feeling curious.

"Don't you remember what happened to you?" said Jack.

"No," I said. "I have no idea what you're talking about."

"Amos found you on the floor in the clinic's car park next to your car," said Jack. "We think you were mugged, although they must have been disturbed before they could take anything. You have actually been unconscious for 5 days, we have been so worried."

"I don't understand," I said. "I can't remember. Surely, I should do if something like that happened to me?"

"The doctor warned us that might be the case," said Amos. "It's quite common with a head injury. Your memory will come back but it might be a slow process. What's the last thing you do remember?"

My head started hurting again; I couldn't take in all I was hearing. I tried to think about my last movements but nothing was coming to mind.

"I don't know. I can't even think why I was at the clinic?" I said. "What day was it? Was I seeing patients?" I asked.

"We had meetings all day," said Amos. "We were discussing the setup of the foundation and discussing the board of Trustees. We'd had a full day and made quite a lot of headway."

I looked at Jack. "I really don't remember any of it. Why can't I remember?" I said to him, looking for some explanation.

"Don't worry," he said. "It will come back to you; I'll tell the police you're not up to seeing them yet. I'll be back in a moment."

With that, he kissed me and left the room.

"You know he has been here every moment since you were brought in," said Amos. "He hasn't left your side; I don't think I have ever seen him so distressed."

"He's lovely I don't know what I would do without him," I said.

Amos smiled at me and looked like he wanted to say something else to me and I had the feeling I was missing something but again the past seemed to be a blank. Oh God, I thought, would my head ever stop hurting?

The next couple of days went by, with me being prodded and probed. I had all sorts of tests and examinations. Doctor Hadley didn't think there would be any lasting effects but wanted me to stay in hospital for a couple of days just to make sure I was recovering well but I started to be fed up of being immobile in bed, I wanted some fresh air and to walk about so I pressurised Jack to speak to the doctor to let him take me home.

The next time Amos visited me, I told him how concerned I was that not even the smallest detail or memory of the day before the blow to my head was returning. I thought that I should be having some sort of flash backs but there was nothing.

"Have you thought that perhaps the experience was so bad your mind is deliberately blanking it out?" he asked.

"I don't know, I am really trying to remember some detail but even events before that day seem to be vague," I answered. "That's why I want to ask you a favour."

"Yes, of course. What is it?" he asked.

"Would you hypnotise me and regress me to help me remember?" I asked. "It might help with something I could tell the police too."

Hypnosis was something we both learnt whilst we were training and had often practiced on each other. I felt completely confident with Amos carrying this type of therapy out.

"As long as you're sure, you could have an adverse reaction and it could set your recovery back."

"You know how to handle that situation if it arose, I'm just getting so frustrated not being able to remember, there's something nagging at me too that I feel is important but I just don' t know what it is."

Amos looked at me as if there was some reluctance on his part but in the end he said yes.

Doctor Hadley asked if he could sit in as it was something that had helped his patients in the past and I did not mind but I asked if Jack could be excluded.

Amos said he would speak to Jack and explain that I needed to be completely relaxed and his presence may hinder that. Little did I know that he really needed to explain to Jack that I would most probably remember our estrangement during the hypnosis and he should tell me before the treatment took place.

So the evening before the session with Amos, Jack came into my room and, holding my hand, told me everything. Firstly, that we had not been living together for several weeks, that I had left and he had not been able to find me and I had refused to answer any of his calls. He reminded me about the photographs in the paper and realised what they looked like but he genuinely did not know what had happened that night. He had gone over the night a hundred times, he could not remember meeting the woman and due to the bad head he suffered from the following morning, he believed his drink had been spiked.

I sat there silently whilst he held my hand and recounted the detail of our lives over the last few months. Silent tears fell from my eyes as he spoke and I suddenly felt a loss I realised I had forgotten since receiving my head injury.

"Please don't cry," he said. "It breaks my heart to know I have hurt you so much, but please believe me, it was not meant and I would do anything to put it right. Please say you will come back home so we can sort this out between us. I can't stand the thought of losing you. I have realised I'm nothing without you."

"I don't know," I said. "I can't believe I didn't remember, although I have felt uncomfortable and I haven't realised the reason why but I do feel now that there was sadness inside me which I couldn't explain. I need you to leave me by myself. I need to think. Please go."

"I'm so sorry," he said. He kissed my forehead and reluctantly left.

Chapter 21

I slept fretfully that night. I tossed and turned, dreaming of screaming fans and photographers with huge flashing cameras going off in my face. Ben and his nurses figured in the dreams along with masked muggers and doctors carrying huge syringes filled with noxious liquids. I woke feeling frightened and alone, wanting Jack's arms around me, making me feel safe and loved. When Amos arrived later in the morning, I felt too upset to go ahead with the hypnosis therapy session.

"So Jack spoke to you then?" he asked.

"Yes, I can't believe I did not remember, although deep inside me, something didn't feel right. Why didn't you tell me?"

"I thought you would realise as soon as you came round," he said. "The longer I left it, the harder it got to say anything. I thought your memory would start coming back slowly. What are you going to do?"

"I don't know," I said. "I don't know what I'm going to do or what I'm thinking. I don't seem to know what's real or if I am in a nightmare that I can't wake up from." I was feeling extremely tearful.

"Take a moment," he said. "If you were one of your patients, what would you suggest to them? You are so good at sorting out other people's problems. Why can't you be that kind to yourself?"

He was right of course, running away like I had was wrong, it solved nothing. Running away from Ben had been the right thing to do. It had taught me that I did not need him to get by. I had learnt I could stand on my own two feet. But it was different with Jack. I loved him so much. When I was without him, I felt as if part of me was missing. We needed to talk through what had happened. Talking was the only way to really sort things through.

"Look," Amos said. "I have a couple of patients I can see whilst I am here, so I'll leave you to get yourself together and I'll come back this afternoon. If you don't want to go ahead with the hypnosis, I'll understand."

"Yes, I do. I'm starting to feel that part of my life is a black hole. I need to remember," I said. "Thank you, Amos, you're a good friend. I'll see you later."

Doctor Hadley came in to see me as soon as Amos left and said he was concerned that I looked so distressed.

"I think you need to spend a couple of more days with us. I'm a bit concerned your recovery is not happening as quickly as I would like," he said.

"No," I said. "I think I need to be home in familiar surroundings. I think that's what I need. I'm going to get up, shower and get properly dressed. I've been in this bed far too long. I'm stagnating."

"Well, that's positive," he said. "Good, I always know when a patient is getting better, they start to tell me what they're going to do instead of taking my advice."

"Sorry," I said.

"No, you carry on. I'll be back this afternoon to sit in on your session with Amos if that's still OK?"

With that, he left and I started to get up and dressed. I was shaky for a while and it seemed to take forever but eventually I was showered, dressed and almost felt quite normal again.

I phoned Jack and suggested he come in the evening so we could talk and I told him I wanted to come home if that was OK with him. I could hear the joy in his voice when he said yes.

"Are you sure?" he asked. "I can't believe you're going to be here again, the place has been empty without you. It's just not the same."

Not having much sleep the night before must have caught up with me and I slept soundly and was only woken by the orderly with a lunch tray.

I felt better, more like my own self and when Amos and Doctor Hadley arrived, I felt ready for the hypnosis session.

The session went well and I remembered the incident, although I did not know who had attacked me as I didn't see the person. I thought I had heard voices and one had sounded like a women's voice asking if I was dead, but Amos said there were several people around me when he arrived on the scene and that is what I might have remembered someone saying that who was at the scene and close to me.

Other memories had returned also. I remembered where I had been staying and I asked Amos to contact Julie, the housekeeper and make sure she knew what was happening to me. But he informed me she had been in touch with him and was fully aware I was in hospital.

Jack arrived at the same time as the police, who wanted to speak to me about the attack. I was able to tell them what I had remembered, which wasn't very much, but they took a statement and said they would be in touch. Evidently, they had some CCTV footage from the scene and this was currently being examined.

When they left me, I felt exhausted.

"You look pale again," said Jack. "Are you sure you're well enough to leave hospital and come home?"

"Are you having second thoughts already?" I asked.

"Never," he said. "I would take you now if I could, carry you out in my arms and I would never let you go again."

I smiled, "I just want to be home in my own bed," I said.

"That's where I want you too," he replied.

Dr Hadley agreed to let me go the following morning, although reluctant at first, he learnt that Jack had hired a nurse for me for as long as needed and he said he would type up some notes about my ongoing treatment for the nurse concerned. A follow up appointment was made for two weeks' time and everything was set for me to go home.

Amos called at the hospital the following morning to say goodbye and told me not to worry about work, everything was ticking over fine and there was nothing of immediate urgency. He said he would speak to me in a few days and perhaps if I was recovering well, we could get together and catch up. I thanked him for everything he had done for me and told him he was a true friend I felt so lucky having him in my life.

Presents arrived for all the staff from Jack. There was a Harrods Hamper for the nurses, a box of fine wines for Dr Hadley and boxes of chocolates for all the other staff. There were hugs and kisses from them all and eventually I was out. Charles was a very welcome sight at the door and opening the car door he said, "So nice to see you, madam." And he looked as though he really meant it.

The journey home did not take long and it felt so good to be outside again. During the journey, Jack never let go of me. Edna and the hired nurse were waiting at the front door.

"I'm glad you're home, madam," said Edna. "Can I introduce you to nurse Joyce Hopkins?" A large young woman with a pleasant round face and deep, dark eyes stepped forward and shook my hand.

"Hello," she said. "Let me take those things for you, your rooms all ready and I bet you would like a nice pot of coffee, wouldn't you?"

I could see we were going to get on fine and over the next few days, we did. She had a naturally sunny deposition. She was always happy, chatted endlessly about everyone she had ever met and when I was fully recovered, I was sorry to see her go.

My recovery was slow. I grew tired very quickly and when tired my head started to ache. I did slowly start to remember things. I would be doing ordinary everyday chores and memories would just pop into my mind. I was still having strange dreams and tossed and turned at night.

The first night I woke at about 2 in the morning to find Jack lying next to me. He was lying on top of the bedclothes. He had decided to let me have the bed to myself and had volunteered to sleep in the guest room until I was feeling better. When I woke, he was just lying there looking at me.

"I'm sorry, I just needed to be by you," he said. "I'm frightened I would wake up and find you gone. The feeling is overwhelming."

"I'm not going anywhere. I don't think I could even if I wanted to," I said.

"You don't want to, do you?" he asked.

"No, I don't," I said, smiling at him. "I'm where I want to be. Now why don't you get into bed and give me a cuddle?"

Our relationship improved over the next few weeks. I think that was because we were talking. He told me about everything he could remember about that dreadful night. He could remember being in the bar of the hotel having a beer with the rest of the band and crew and although he had not had a lot to drink, he could remember very little else.

He woke up in the morning with a bad head, alone in his room and it was not until later the following day when he was shown the pictures in the paper that he realised anyone had been with him. He said he didn't recognise the women in the pictures and had asked the others that had been in the bar if they recognised her, but no one could remember her.

It was after this conversation that I remembered consulting the private detective. I wondered if he had been trying to get in touch with me and I decided to get in touch with him.

Before I had a chance to do this, Charles spoke to me about him. I had asked to speak to Charles and he came into my little sitting room one morning soon after my coming home.

"Hello, Charles, please come in and sit down I have a task for you," I said.

He seemed out of place in this small room and was such a large man he filled the space.

"Yes, madam," he said. "How can I help?"

"This is the address of the place I have been staying the last couple of weeks," I said handing him a piece of paper with the address of Keith and Elaine's Gloucestershire home.

"I have spoken to the housekeeper there. Her name is Julie, she has kindly packed up all my things and when you have free time, would you go and collect them? I have included her telephone number so she is expecting your call when you are on your way."

"Yes, madam," he said. "No problem, I can most probably go tomorrow morning unless Mr Jack needs me for anything."

"Thank you," I replied.

He got up to leave but hesitated.

"Is there something else?" I asked.

"I do realise that you are not a 100% recovered but my friend Jason Allan has been trying to get in touch with you," he said.

"Jason Allan?" I enquired.

"Yes," he replied. "He's the friend of mine you consulted just before I took you to the airport when you left. I explained to him what had happened to you and he has asked me to speak to you to arrange a meeting with him when you feel well enough."

"I have remembered I spoke to someone but I could not remember his name and to tell you the truth, the meeting I had with him is a bit vague still, but I do need to see him. If you have his number, I will give him a ring."

At that, he wrote down the number and passed it to me.

"Thank you, Charles," I said, taking the number from him. "I'm sorry if I have put you in any trouble."

"You could never do that, madam," he said. "We have all been so concerned about you. I'm glad you're making a recovery."

"Thank you."

Chapter 22

That evening I told Jack about Jason Allan.

"Have you spoken to him?" he asked. "Does he know anything?"

"I haven't spoken to him yet," I said. "But I want you to be with me when I do speak to him."

"Of course, I want to be with you, I need to know what happened too."

"What if it implicates you? If I found out you have been telling me lies, my world will fall apart," I said, with tears welling up inside of me.

"I promise you I have told you everything I remember. I wouldn't knowingly ever hurt you. Please believe me."

"I'll phone him in the morning and ask him to come here," I said. "I still don't feel up to travelling about."

"OK," agreed Jack. "Let's hope he has been able to find something out that will shred a light on what happened."

When I spoke to Jason Allan, he informed me that he had collected a lot of information to discuss with me.

"Can you call to see me at home?" I asked. "I am still not a hundred per cent and I don't feel happy about being out and about."

"That's understandable, it's fine," he said. "How about tomorrow morning about 10.30, is that OK with you?"

"Yes, that's OK," I replied. "There is something else I need to tell you."

"What's that?" asked Jason.

"I have told my husband that I consulted you and he will be with me when we meet tomorrow."

"That's fine, as long as you are happy with that," he said. "I am sure what I have to say will be very interesting to him, too."

"We'll see you tomorrow then," I said.

"Look forward to it," he replied.

I told Jack about the appointment and what Jason had to say. He was quiet and then said, "I hope it clears the matter up once and for all. This has nearly destroyed us and I can never forgive anyone that brought it about."

We were both apprehensive about the following day and when Edna brought Jason Allan into the room Jack was holding my hand so tightly, I thought he would break my fingers.

"Jason," I said, "This is my husband Jack. Jack, this is Jason Allan, Charles' friend."

"How do you do?" said Jason, shaking Jack's hand. "I'm a great fan."

"Thank you," said Jack.

Jason then turned to me and shook my hand. "I'm sorry to hear about your attack Mrs London I hope you're feeling better?" he said. "Do the police know who did it?"

"They're still investigating the incident," said Jack. "Please take a seat. Can we get you a coffee?"

"That would be great," he replied.

Edna poured us all a coffee and left us with our visitor.

"I think the information I have to give you is going to come as a bit of a shock," Jason said looking concerned as he took papers and what looked like photographs from his briefcase. "You are going to ask me questions about what I have to say and that is fine but I would appreciate that I finish my report before you start asking questions that way, I don't get waylaid and miss out something important." He waited a few seconds whilst we both nodded our agreement.

"Firstly, Mrs London, you asked me to identify the woman in the photographs that appeared in the papers. This I was able to do quite quickly. In fact, I think she is known to you, Mr London," said Jason, looking at Jack.

"I must admit she does look familiar but I can't place her or where I know her from," said Jack, looking at me and holding my hand tighter than ever.

"Her name is Simone McKenzie," said Jason.

"No," said Jack. "I don't recognise the name."

"Her father owns the company 'McKenzie Logistics', I think they're the company you use that are in charge of ensuring all your stage equipment gets to the right place when you're touring."

"Yes, that's right," said Jack. "We've used them for years, I know Bill McKenzie very well. Of course, I know Simone, she's very often backstage with the other stage hands but I have never really taken that much notice of her."

"Well, she's taken notice of you," said Jason. "She's had an obsessive crush on you since she was a teenager and she believes you feel the same way about her."

"But that's ridiculous, I hardly know her."

"From what I gather, her obsession has been growing over a number of years and it's got to a dangerous stage, so much so that Mrs London is now her focus. She believes that Mrs London is the person that is stopping you, Mr London and her being together."

"How do you know this?" I asked.

"I've managed to speak to her, get to know her, I have been following her for several weeks now and found out a lot about her life, but please let me go on and complete my report."

Jack let go of my hand and put his arm around me. I think we were both apprehensive about what Jason was going to reveal.

"The evening in question seems to have been very well planned in advance. Simone had an accomplice, who I believe spiked your drink in the bar that night. I have spoken to several people that were around who saw two people, a man and woman, helping you to your room that night thinking you were worse for drink and although they realised it was most unlike you, the people, one of them being Simone, were well known to them, so they did not think anything of it."

"An accomplice? Who?" asked Jack. "It must have been someone I knew well enough to get close to me to be able to spike my drink. Who was it?"

"That's the second thing your wife wanted me to find out. I'll come to that later, but I think it was him that took the photos and subsequently sold them to the newspapers."

"I find it very hard to believe anyone hates us enough to cause this much upset to us," I said.

"Oh, believe it, Mrs London, both of them wanted to inflict as much harm and upset as they possibly could. They both hate the relationship you have together, your successful careers and financial status is a source of great envy to them both."

I turned to Jack and said, "I'm sorry I should have trusted you. When I think how close I came to walking away from you because of this, they almost achieved what they wanted."

"I feel so stupid," said Jack. "To think I could allow anyone to do this. It must have been someone I was close to."

We both looked at Jason, wanting to hear more of what he was going to tell us.

"I have been following Simone and her accomplice for the past several weeks and I know that both of them were in the vicinity of the car park where you were attacked, Mrs London," said Jason.

"What?" said Jack. "Are you saying these two people were responsible for the attack on my wife?"

"I can think of no other reason why they would have been there," said Jason. "It's a private car park for the clinic and I have pictures of them leaving in great haste after the attack."

"Let me have a look at the photos I may be able to recognise Simone's accomplice," said Jack.

Jason started to look through the papers he had in front of him and pulling one out, he said to Jack. "I am sure you will know exactly who it is."

Jack picked up the photo and looked at it fully for a second or two, as if he could not quite believe what he was seeing.

"Who is it?" I asked.

Jack passed me the photo, putting his hand to his mouth in disbelief.

I looked at the photo of a man in a hooded jacket. He was tall with fair hair. The photo was very clear and I quickly realised who I was looking at. "Stephen," I said. "I don't know why you're surprised," I said, looking at Jack. "It's not the first time he's attacked me."

"I think your brother is a dangerous man, Mr London and the sooner I hand this information over to the police the safer you and your family will be," said Jason, collecting the papers and files that were spread out in front of us.

"No," said Jack. "We will deal with this ourselves."

"Oh no, we won't!" I said with a slightly raised voice. "This ends now. You convinced me the first time he attacked me not to go to the police and look how that's turned out. I was left for dead after this attack. Don't you see how serious this is, Jack?"

"The publicity will be horrendous," said Jack, clutching my hand. "Every bit of our personal lives will be put under scrutiny and be reported in the papers whether there's any truth in it or not."

"No, Jack, not this time," I said, almost shouting at him now. "If you don't care about me enough to do this, I will go to the police with Jason whether you like it or not."

At that I got up and strode out of the room, shaking and not being able to trust myself to say anything else.

"I think your wife is right, Mr London. This is obviously not the first time your brother has been violent and personally, I don't think it will be the last. I cannot let this information be forgotten I am duty bound to report what I believe is someone breaking the law to be reported to the police."

"Yes, of course, you are right," said Jack, looking very crestfallen. "You and my wife are correct, we should go to the police. He's my brother though, you know and I have tried to do right by him, although he has never appreciated it. He has always blamed me for being successful and leaving him behind but it was never anything I consciously did to scupper his career. His resentment has just grown worse and worse over the years."

"There's something else that has happened in the past week that you should be aware of."

"What's that?" asked Jack.

"Your brother and Simone were married last week. They are now husband and wife."

Jack just nodded. "Will you contact the police and then they can contact us?" he asked Jason.

"Yes, I am sure they will be in touch."

Jack shook hands with Jason and showed him out.

"Give my regards to Mrs London," Jason said. "Will you inform her of your decision to tell the police?"

"Yes," said Jack. "Thank you for everything."

It was only a few minutes after Jason had left that Jack came into the bedroom where I was sat, trying to calm myself down.

"I'm sorry," he said as he entered the room. "I don't know what I was thinking."

"Of yourself as usual and how any publicity may affect your fan base," I said rather sharply.

"How could you say that?"

"They left me for dead, Jack; you could be arranging my funeral at this moment instead of being concerned about what the papers might say."

"Please don't say that. I don't think I could carry on without you. You are everything to me. The weeks you were away were hellish. This house was empty without you. Please, I've told Jason to contact the police and give them all the information he has."

I sat quietly, not replying to him. He came and sat next to me and put his arm around me.

"I'm sorry," he said again but I didn't reply. My head was hurting and I just wanted to lie down in the quiet and go over all the information Jason had given us.

"Can you ask Joyce to come in? I think it's time for my medicine, my head has started to hurt."

"Yes, of course," he said, looking concerned. "Is there anything else I can get you?"

I shook my head and he left the room.

I did not manage to think over what Jason had told us as I slipped into a restful sleep soon after taking the medication Joyce had given me and when I woke, I felt a little better. Joyce came into the bedroom and informed me that lunch was ready. "Would you like it here on a tray?" she asked.

"No, I'll come down. Just give me a few moments to tidy up and I'll be right down."

Jack was already in the room when I arrived.

"Jason Allan has been on the telephone to say he's been to the police and they will want to talk to us in the next few days."

"Good," I said and silently sat and ate lunch, not feeling I could trust myself to talk to him about the events of the morning without getting upset.

Jason phoned me later that evening, making sure I was OK. I thanked him for being so thoughtful.

"I was concerned about you, Mrs London," he said. "You did not look at all well. I'm sure the information you received from me this morning must have been very distressing."

"Yes it was," I replied. "But we need now to come to terms about what has happened and move forward."

"I think you're right but I have a feeling not everything has come to light yet," he said.

"Well, I hope you're wrong I don't think we can take much more bad news."

Chapter 23

The rest of the day, I was restless and did not feel well. My head ached and I decided to rest in bed. Jack took himself off to the studio and shut himself away. I took another dose of painkillers and as soon as my head touched the pillow, I was asleep.

Joyce came into the room just before dinner but found she was unable to wake me. She made sure I was breathing, put me in the recovery position and then called Dr Hadley who immediately arranged for an ambulance to have me re-admitted back into hospital as quickly as possible.

"Edna, Edna," Joyce called down the stairs.

"What is it, Joyce? Is something wrong?" Edna asked, coming to the bottom of the stairs.

"It's Mrs London, I can't wake her. I've called Dr Hadley and he's sending an ambulance. Can you get Mr London to come?" asked Joyce.

"Oh, my goodness!" exclaimed Edna. "I'll fetch him straight away."

Jack was beside me in seconds and tried to wake me, to no avail.

It took the ambulance 19 minutes to get to the house and within a further 10 minutes, I was on my way to the hospital.

Dr Hadley assessed me immediately and I was sent for an MRI scan. Jack was anxious to find out how I was and if I was in danger, but it was some time before Dr Hadley could speak to him. Jack was beside my bed when Dr Hadley finally came to speak to him.

"Hello, Mr London, I'm so sorry to see you back here so soon," he said, shaking Jack's hand.

"How is she? Is she going to be alright?" Jack asked. "She seemed fine this morning, although she had a headache."

"Well, it looks like Mrs London has had a slight bleed on the brain, which has left a small blood clot. We are treating this and for the time being, we think it would be best if she remains in an induced coma to help her recovery."

"How long will this be for?" asked Jack.

"We're not sure, we will monitor her constantly and hopefully she will improve enough over the next few days to be brought out of the coma and hopefully make a full recovery."

"And if not, what might happen?"

"Let's see what the next 24 hours bring. We are hopeful everything will be OK."

Jack stayed with me and even slept in a made-up bed in the hospital room. He was extremely distressed, believing that he was partially to blame for the current state I was in. He believed he had put me under pressure when he told me he did not want to report Stephen to the police. The longer I stayed in a coma, the worse he felt.

A further MRI was carried out on the second day and it was decided to let me come out of the induced coma.

Late on the third day, I woke up. Jack, Dr Hadley and a nurse were in my room.

"Hello, Mrs London, how are you feeling?" asked Dr Hadley.

"Not sure. Where am I?" I asked.

"We had to bring you back into hospital as we couldn't wake you," I recognised Jack's voice.

"Oh my goodness, is everything alright now? Am I OK now?"

"Well, we need to run some more tests and keep a close eye on your progress but at the moment everything looks positive and I think you should make a full recovery," said Dr Hadley in a positive manner. "I insist, however, that you stay here in hospital until we are satisfied you are completely recovered. Is that agreed, Mrs London?"

I nodded my head, which I immediately regretted, as the pain in my head was excruciating.

"Well, I think you should now get some rest perhaps nurse will arrange for you to have something to eat and drink and your visitor should leave and get some rest himself," Dr Hadley suggested looking at Jack.

"Can I come back in the morning?" Jack asked.

Dr Hadley nodded and Jack kissed me on the forehead and said he would be back first thing in the morning.

I stayed a further 2 weeks in hospital and felt completely well when I left. Jack and I had instructions that I was to have a complete rest with no resuming work for at least a month. Jack wanted to take me away on holiday but I was advised not to fly and anyway I just wanted to be at home and sleep in my own bed.

Joyce, my nurse, had been retained to ensure I rested completely and to my surprise when I arrived home Julie was standing in as housekeeper as Edna had gone to look after her sister in Bournemouth as she had fallen and broken her hip. Elaine and Keith had finally sold the house in the Cotswolds and Julie was between jobs when Jack needed to cover Edna's absence. Unbeknown to either of us, Charles had struck up a friendship with Julie when they met and had suggested to Jack that she could step into help whilst Edna was away.

So I arrived home to a warm welcome and lots of hugs and smiles. It was so good to be back in my own bed. I showered and changed into my night wear but went downstairs and lay wrapped up on the sofa. Jack was so solicitous offering me everything he could think of to make me comfortable. We had discussed how he felt after I had become ill again but I assured him it wasn't his fault that I had been unlucky and it couldn't be foreseen that I would have a relapse.

The police had been to see Jack whilst I had been in hospital and they had tried to contact both Stephen and Simone but they had fled the country and at the moment were untraceable. At some time they would need to speak to me but Jack had managed to keep them away for the moment.

Chapter 24

Our lives changed during this time. I had spent so long away from work that I realised that, for some time, work was no longer the focus of my life. I didn't need it like I use to. Also Jack, although still writing and recording, He no longer wanted to tour. He still did one off concerts but they tended to be closer to home and he rarely travelled abroad. If he did, he was away only a few days and we both made a conscious effort to spend more time together and get our relationship back on track.

We became lovers again; I had missed him so much and I came to understand that the encounter with Simone was not of his making. We talked endlessly about what had happened and both of us realised we wanted to be with each other more than anything else and could not imagine either of us being without the other.

Eventually, I was given the OK to travel and we opened up the house in Portugal, as I did not want to be far away. The summer was practically over but the approaching autumn brought softer sunnier days and cooler nights. We took Joyce with us, Jack insisted on it and Julie came too, so I was looked after and cosseted better than anyone could wish for. I sat in the sunshine and after three weeks when we returned home, I had a lovely colour and looked and felt so much better.

As always when Jack had time on his hands he sat and wrote, so by the time we returned home he had enough material for a new album and work started in the studio almost as soon as we were home.

Whilst we had been away, Charles with the advice of Jason Allan had updated the whole of our security systems. There were now sensors over the grounds and panic buttons installed in the house. Extra security personnel had been employed and Jack insisted that if I left the house, I should always be accompanied.

"Can I have a word, Mrs London?" said Joyce, coming into the sitting room with morning coffee soon after we had arrived back home.

"Yes, of course," was my reply. "How can I help? Please take a seat."

"Thank you," she said, sitting down beside me. "I think it's about time I moved on. You seem to be completely recovered now and I am finding that I do not have enough to keep me busy."

"Oh, Joyce, I shall miss you, but you are right and hopefully when I see Dr Hadley tomorrow, he will sign me off. I completely understand your need to be busy and I am sure you have no lack of offers for your nursing services."

"Thank you. I have enjoyed working for you and will miss you all very much," Joyce answered.

"Well, OK then, If Dr Hadley signs me off tomorrow I will reluctantly let you go. We will pay you until the end of the month if that is OK with you?"

"That's more than generous. Thank you, Mrs London," she rose and held out her hand.

I stood up also and shook hands with her, realising I would miss her terribly.

I went back to my coffee, suddenly feeling lonely and thought I had been missing contact with my friends and had been neglecting so many of them. So much so, I spent the rest of the morning phoning friends and catching up with all sorts of news.

Jack came in for lunch, which was unusual as when he was in the studio, he would work straight through the day.

"Hi, how are you feeling?" he asked, kissing me on the forehead.

"I feel absolutely fine," I replied. "In fact, I have been speaking to Joyce and if Dr Hadley signs me off tomorrow, we have agreed that she should leave to find another situation."

"Are you sure?" he asked.

"Yes, I think she is a little bored with so little to do now I have recovered."

"As long as you are sure, but make sure Dr Hadley is OK with it," he said. "What have you been doing with yourself?"

"Just catching up with people," I said. "I have asked dad over for the weekend, it seems so long since we have been together and I thought I would ask Amos and John for lunch on Sunday as I need to speak to Amos about the business."

"I don't want you going back to work yet. Please wait until we can speak to Dr Hadley tomorrow," asked Jack earnestly.

"Well, actually I was going to speak to Amos about retiring completely from the business and finding out how he felt about it and asking him how he wanted to continue."

"Really?" Jack said, surprised. "I am pleased if that is what you want. It means we can spend more time together, but it has to be what you truly want. Are you sure you won't be bored without seeing your patients?"

"I thought I could concentrate on my writing again and we could have more time to spend together, yes I have been thinking about it for some time and it is what I want. That's the decision I have come to and I am determined to carry it out."

So during the afternoon, I spoke to Amos and asked him and John for lunch the following Sunday. I also explained that we needed a little time during the day to discuss the future, which Amos agreed to.

"You must be feeling better," Amos said. "That's the first time in weeks you have mentioned the business to me."

"I'm sorry," I apologised. "I realise that I have left you dealing with everything, but Dr Hadley still hasn't okayed me to come back to work."

"Don't worry, I fully understand how ill you have been," said Amos. "It hasn't been a problem. All your patients were coming to the end of their treatment and the ones that have needed longer term have been happy to see someone else."

"Thank you. I appreciate all you have done for me. I truly do."

So the weekend was planned and to make it complete, Wills phoned and asked if he could come for the weekend and bring a friend called Emily. This was unusual as although Wills came to stay for a few weekends when he was able, He had never brought anyone with him before.

Chapter 25

Dad arrived on Friday afternoon and it was so good to see him. As he no longer drove, Charles had collected him. He had visited me several times whilst I was in hospital and was now pleased I was fully recovered. Julie asked if he liked anything in particular and subsequently we dined on homemade Venison casserole with red cabbage and chocolate pudding for afters.

If Julie was going to be with us much longer, I realised I needed to up my exercise regime.

Wills and Emily arrived late on Friday night. She was a delightful young woman with long fair hair, grey-green eyes and the prettiest smile. I could see straight away that Wills was smitten. After they had settled into their room, they had a late kitchen supper and joined Jack and me in the big sitting room. Emily seemed over awed by Jack and hung on his every word. I remembered how I had reacted all those years ago when I had first come to this house and I understood how she must be feeling.

"You have a lovely house, Mrs London," she said.

Jack offered to give her a tour and I asked him not to spend ages talking about his guitar collection. He smiled as if he too was remembering that night long ago. Whilst they were away, I was able to interrogate Wills about Emily.

"So tell me all about her," I asked. "Where did you meet?"

"She came into A and E with her little boy and we just seemed to click straight away," Wills answered. "She's lovely, don't you think?"

"Yes, she is. How old is her little boy?"

"He's almost two. I'd like to bring him with us next time if that's alright?"

"That would be lovely. Please feel free to fill the place with children, I would be delighted."

"Well, if she will have me, that's what I intend to do."

"I am so pleased, Wills. We could do with some happiness and a celebration. This calls for champagne."

"Well, let's not be too previous, she may not have me."

"Don't be ridiculous, she doesn't look stupid."

We were both still laughing when Jack and Emily came back into the room.

"What are you laughing about?" asked Jack.

"I'm enjoying the company of family and I want some champagne to celebrate," I said.

"Champagne?" queried Jack. "Well, why not."

"That sounds lovely," said Emily.

So we stayed up rather late, talking, laughing and drinking champagne to the early hours.

Subsequently, we were all late arriving at the breakfast table the next morning. Jack suggested a walk in the woods to get rid of the cobwebs. So after breakfast, we donned coats and walking boots, collected the dogs and set off for the woods. Dad stayed behind to read the papers, but we all set off not too briskly to start with but were soon in the woods and enjoying the fresh air.

"That's strange," said Wills. "Looks like someone has been camping here look, the ground is flattened and there have been a couple of fires lit."

"Yes," said Jack, looking at the place where Wills was standing.

"It must be some fans trying to get a glimpse at their favourite rock star," I said, not quite believing in my assumption.

"I'll get Charles and the security guys to check it out," said Jack. "Come on let's get back and have coffee. My mouth feels like the bottom of a birdcage."

After coffee, Emily asked if we minded if she had a lie down as the night before festivities were catching up on her. None of us minded and it gave us time to discuss the possibility of intruders being in the woods with Charles also filling Wills in about the recent findings about Stephen.

Jack and Charles decided to step up patrols in the woods and it was decided to hire some private security firm. The rest of the day passed quietly and after watching a film in the evening, we all decided to have an early night.

Soon after breakfast had been cleared away the next day, Amos and John arrived. I was surprised at the way John looked. He had lost a lot of weight, looked gaunt and grey, a mere shadow of his former self.

"The cancer is back," Amos said when we were alone in my little sitting room later.

"I'm so sorry, Amos," I said. "I've been so caught up in myself I haven't given a thought to anything that's been affecting you."

"That's not your fault. What could you have done?"

"Supported you," I said. "What's the prognosis?"

"It's not good. We're starting another round of chemotherapy next week but you've seen him. He's so weak."

"What can I do to help?" I asked.

"Well, I will need some time off, but in all honesty the clinics are running without us now that I don't think it will be a problem."

"That's something I wanted to talk to you about. I want to retire from the business completely. I am happy to stay on the board and work on the foundation but would like to retire from seeing patients. Is that something you would agree to?"

"Whole heartedly," he said. "Both of us have become more like administrators than therapists and if in the future if we feel we want to, we can set up in Harley Street and see a few private patients."

"OK, shall we contact our lawyers and notify the Canadians officially?"

"Yes, I'll set up an appointment tomorrow."

"I'm sorry, Amos, but we have been very successful and can walk away with our heads held high and concentrate on our personal lives. We should be able to enjoy our success and look to our futures."

We embraced and kissed each other. I felt it was the end of an era but I knew I would always have a best friend in Amos forever.

I was quiet during lunch but everyone else chatted, laughed, enjoying each other's company. Amos and John left very soon after lunch as John looked tired and Charles took dad back home soon after whilst it was still light. Wills and Emily left after tea but promised to come again very soon bringing Emily's son Logan with them on the next visit.

During the evening, I told Jack about the conversation I had with Amos and he was sorry to hear about John but had realised on seeing him that he was not well. I think it made us both realise how lucky we were to have each other. I also told him that Wills was intending to ask Emily to marry him, which he was delighted about. Life felt good but in some way a little sad at the same time. We made love that night and clung to each other afterwards, shutting the rest of the world out.

Chapter 26

Emily said yes to Wills' proposal and they became officially engaged. Her parents gave them an engagement party to which we were invited. Emily's father had a small manufacturing business in South London and they lived in Surrey. It was a small intimate party, just close family and a few friends.

Emily's mom, Joan, said she had always been a huge fan of Jack's and she enjoyed introducing him to everyone all night long. Jack took it all in his stride and tried very hard not to steal the limelight away from Wills and Emily but if they noticed he was drawing more attention than them they did not show it. Emily's little boy Logan was allowed to stay up later than usual and it was evident that he already loved Wills who hardly ever let go of him. It was good to see him so obviously happy.

"You're quiet," said Will's, finding me stood by myself later in the evening. "What are you thinking about?"

"I'm sorry, I was miles away."

"I know that look. You were thinking about Chrissy, weren't you?" said Wills.

"You know me so well. I'm sorry; I didn't mean to put a damper on the night."

"You haven't," he said, taking my hand and gently kissing me on the cheek. "She should be here with us; she would have loved Emily and Logan. It's times like these that I miss her the most."

"I know, so do I," I replied.

"Wills, come and see the cake," said the little voice of Logan. "It's blue with writing on it; mommy says it says yours and her names. Come and see." By now, he was tugging Wills' hand and pulling him away.

Wills smiled at me and allowed himself to be ushered to see the engagement cake.

The sad moment passed and we did not mention it again. The party continued with flowing champagne and cake and we left in the early hours after thoroughly enjoying ourselves.

It was late when we arrived back home and we went straight to bed, but despite being tired, I could not sleep. I tossed and turned and to make it worse, Jack fell asleep as soon as his head touched the pillow and slept soundly. I must have finally slipped into a deep sleep and was very groggy when the phone rang very early the next morning. I wanted to ignore it and stay asleep but managed to pick up the receiver and, still only half awake, said, "Hello."

"He's gone," the voice at the other end of the phone said.

"Pardon?" I replied.

"He's gone," I now recognised Amos' voice. "It happened in the night. He was fine when we went to bed, although he had had a treatment during the day and was very tired and weak but he was OK."

"Wait, I'm sorry, Amos, I'm still half asleep. Who's gone?" I said very stupidly.

"John, he died during the night. I heard him coughing and go to the bathroom. I asked if he was OK and he said yes, go back to sleep and I did. We have been sleeping in separate bedrooms because I did not like to disturb him when I got up early in the morning. When I went in to take him some coffee this morning, he was dead."

"Oh, Amos, I am so sorry. Do you want me to come over?"

"I don't know what I want. I am so lost. I thought we would get through this. What am I going to do without him?"

"I'll be over as soon as I can. I'm so sorry," I said and as I put the phone down, I could hear him start to sob.

"What's the matter?" said Jack, rousing himself. "Where are you going?"

"I have to go to Amos," I said. "John's passed away in the night."

"What?" he said, surprised. "You can't drive yourself. You're still most probably over the limit from last night and I want you to be safe. I don't want you being out alone."

"Yes, you have a point. I hate to have to wake Charles so early in the morning."

"I'll give him a ring whilst you get ready," Jack offered, getting unsteadily out of bed.

"Thanks."

By the time I had washed and dressed, there was a hot cup of coffee on the table by the side of the bed.

"Charles is ready when you are," Jack said. "Do you want me to come with you?" he asked.

"No, I will be fine. He sounded so upset and in shock on the phone."

"Well, I will come with you if you want me to, but I have some of the boys coming over to talk about a new album. But tell him I'm so sorry, if there is anything he needs, ask him to let us know. Ask him if he would like to come and stay for a few days?"

"I will. I know he'll appreciate the offer. I will ring you later," I said, kissing him on the cheek.

"Take care," he shouted after me as I left the room.

With that, I left waving goodbye as I walked to the waiting car.

"Sorry to get you up so early Charles," I said, stepping in through the open car door.

"It's no problem, madam," Charles replied. "I'm sorry to hear about Mr Amos's friend. It must have hit him hard."

"Yes, I think it has. He sounded devastated on the phone."

The journey continued with very little further conversation and within the hour, we had arrived at Amos and John's home. It was a modern barn conversation with large glass windows from floor to ceiling on the whole part of the front of the house. Amos and John had lived here almost ten years and when they bought the property, it had been little more than a farm barn. With John's flair for design, it had soon been transferred to the property it now was. The glass wall took advantage of the views to the front of the property, which was open countryside with no other properties in sight.

As soon as I stepped out of the car, Amos opened one of the large oak front doors and came over to me, hugging me tightly and sobbing. This was so unlike him he was usually in control of his emotions but was obviously overwhelmed by his loss.

"Oh Amos, please don't, it's so sad to see you like this," I said, holding him close to me.

"I'm so sorry; I just don't seem to be able to help myself." I feel like my insides have been ripped out of me the pain is so physical.

"I know. I'm so sorry he was such a lovely person. I shall miss him so much."

"I don't think I can live without him."

"Come, let's go inside and have a warm drink and sit and talk."

Amos just nodded and continued to cling to me until we were inside. I made us a pot of tea and we sat and talked; first about what had happened and then about John. Amos eventually calmed a little but little sobs still emerged whilst we talked.

"Jack asks if you would like to come and stay with us for a little while, as we don't feel you should be by yourself."

"No, that's fine, thank you, but I have things that I will need to deal with and John's sister is coming over to stay," Amos replied. "She'll be here later today."

"Well, if that's what you want but I'll stay with you until she arrives if you like."

"Thank you. I don't think I want to be by myself just now," he said.

It was a long day and the time passed so slowly. Amos told me that although John had been ill for such a long time, he was expected to make a good recovery. The prognosis had seemed good and although at first the treatment of chemotherapy had made John very sick and was extremely debilitating; the Oncologist had adjusted the drugs being used and John had started to tolerate the treatment better.

The suddenness of his death was heart breaking. Talking about it helped Amos but he suddenly started sobbing it was so raw.

John's sister Janine arrived during the early evening. She seemed a sensible woman and although very distraught herself, she immediately took charge of Amos and clinging to her, he seemed to calm a little. I didn't realise that her and John were twins and I couldn't understand why I knew so little about John's life. Amos had always supported me so much and had always been on hand whenever I needed a true friend why hadn't I been there for him in the same way.

I suddenly felt guilty, my life with Jack was all-consuming in so many ways there was little room for anything else. I resolved to spend more time thinking about my friends and family and just how much they meant to me.

Amos succumbed to Janine's no-nonsense attitude and I felt happy leaving him in her capable hands. In lots of ways she was very much like John, she sounded like him when she spoke and after a very short time, I could recognise some of John's traits in her.

I felt utterly drained and looked forward to being home again with Jack. If one thing today had taught me was that you should make every moment count because in the blink of an eye, everything can change.

Charles had waited for me all day and I was so pleased to be on our way.

As we drove down the drive at home and arrived at the front of the house, Charles queried, "Hello, what's going on here then?"

"Pardon," I said, rousing myself from the drowsy state I had been in most of the way home.

"There are police cars here. I hope nothing has happened whilst we have been away," said Charles, sounding slightly anxious.

I was now wide awake and could see two police cars parked outside the front of the house.

"Jack," I shouted as I stepped from the car. I suddenly had a sense of dread but then could see Jack stood in the doorway shaking hands with one of the policemen.

"It's OK, nothing to worry about," Jack said reassuringly as he stepped across to me. "I'll explain everything to you inside. How's Amos?"

"Well, he's not OK but John's sister has arrived to stay with him so he's not by himself," I replied. "Why are the police here? What's been happening?"

"Come inside and you, Charles. You will need to hear what's been happening here today."

We went into the sitting room and Jack poured us all a drink. Julie came in and asked if we had eaten. Jack said he had waited for me so we decided on a light late supper and Julie went away and said it would be ready in thirty minutes.

"So come on then," I said to Jack. "Tell us what has been happening?"

"Stephen was here!" Jack said.

"What? How?" I said incredulously.

"He was waiting for me in the studio this morning when I went in there."

"How on earth did he get in?" exclaimed Charles. "We have more security here than they have at the Tower of London protecting the Crown Jewels. Christ!"

"You forget, he lived here a long time. He knows every inch of this place, perhaps better than either of us," said Jack.

"Did he hurt you?" I asked. "What did he want?"

"He said he wanted to talk. I really didn't recognise him at first. He looked awful and you could tell he was terrified of Simone. He didn't seem to be in his right mind. He wasn't making any sense at all."

"You sound sorry for him," I said quietly. "Jack, they tried to kill me. As far as they were concerned, I was dead. They left me lying on that garage floor believing I was dead."

"I know, I know. I could never forgive him and I told him that. He said he wasn't in his right mind he didn't know what he was doing," Said, Jack holding me close to him and kissing my forehead.

"Where is he now?" I asked.

"I don't know I told him I was phoning the police and he rushed out screaming he was sorry."

Charles got up. "I'm going to get everyone out there looking. I want to make sure he's gone. Try not to worry we will all be on high alert tonight. He won't get in again."

"Thank you, Charles," I said, also standing up. "Make sure you come back to have something to eat."

With that, he disappeared from the room.

"What else did he say?" I asked.

"He was rambling about a lot of things. He said he had got involved with her fanatical obsession with me and because of his hatred of me, believing I had taken everything from him, he was too involved before he realised what he was doing. He said at first he wanted to make me suffer and that's what the setup with the photographs in the paper were all about but when he found out what she was prepared to do, what she had already done, he was horrified and just wanted to extricate himself but she wouldn't let him."

"What did he mean? What had she already done?"

"He didn't say."

"Why did he marry her if she was so terrifying?"

"He thought he had found a soulmate, someone like him that had an axe to grind, someone who hated me as much as he did. But he quickly realised she didn't hate me she was obsessed with me and hated everyone that stood between me and her, anyone that was stopping us being together."

Jack poured us another drink and I suddenly realised I had emptied my glass a bit too quickly.

"He really wasn't making much sense," Jack went on. "He kept saying 'You don't know what she's done, but I didn't know I really didn't know you have to believe me.' I couldn't get out of him what he was talking about. He sounded as if he was losing his mind. When I said about calling the police, he said there was no need, it was going to be alright now that's what he had come to tell me. With that he run out, I tried to follow him but he was like something demented so I just called the police and I think it's best left to them now."

"Oh Jack, do you think he's still around? Will he come back?" I asked, feeling anxious about the fact that no one knew how he had got in and where he had disappeared to.

"No, I think he is definitely gone. Please don't worry. I'll ask Charles to have a couple of the security people stay inside the house tonight. I'm so sorry you have had to come back to all this after the day you have had. You look washed out why don't we have an early night after supper."

"I do feel drained," I said, feeling quite exhausted. "Although, I think I shall toss and turn all night my mind is racing with all you have told me."

In the end I fell into a deep sleep as soon as my head touched the pillow and I was awoken quite late by Jack bringing me a tray with breakfast.

Chapter 27

"You seem to have slept well after all," he said. "You must have been exhausted. Are you feeling better?"

"Yes, thank you. What time is it?" I replied, rubbing my eyes open and slowly sitting up.

"It's gone nine. I wanted you to sleep as long as you could," kissing me on the forehead.

"Thanks, Jack. Were there any sightings of Steven overnight?"

"No, nothing, but there seem to be a lot of people out there searching everywhere," he said, getting up off the bed and going towards the window.

I sat up and poured a cup of coffee and watched Jack at the window. He seemed a million miles away, deep in thought and stayed like that for several minutes, then suddenly seemed to come back to the here and now. He walked back over to the bed and picked up a piece of toast that I had just buttered.

"You know you look lovely with your hair all tousled after being asleep," he said, smiling and munching on my toast.

"Thanks, but I can't imagine that I do."

"I do love you so, I don't know what I would do without you," he said, kissing me again and leaving toast crumbs on my lips.

"I love you too, but I must get up I have a lot to do today."

"Oh, I think whatever you have to do can wait a little bit longer," he said, pulling his jumper up over his head. "Move over I want seconds."

Sometime later, with my bed hair even more tousled, I got up, showered and dressed ready to face the day.

On my way downstairs, the telephone rang and I answered it to find Edna calling. We spoke for some considerable time and when we had finished, I went to find Jack, who was in the studio listening to the latest recording the group had been working on.

"Hi Darling, have you come for thirds?" he enquired with a cheeky grin on his face.

"No, I haven't, you reprobate. What on earth have you had for breakfast you're very frisky this morning?"

"I had you. Surely, you haven't forgotten already?"

"Oh, stop it, I have something serious to discuss."

"Really, this early in the morning? Can't it wait for an hour I'm right in the middle of something?"

"I thought you were quite willing to stop what you were doing a second ago."

"Well, that was a better incentive than a serious talk."

"You're incorrigible, but don't leave it too long. Come in for coffee. I'll be in the sitting room," I said, kissing him on the top of his head as he had already turned back to the console table he was sitting at.

Julie had just brought coffee in when Jack arrived.

"Thank you, Julie, that's just what I need," he said, thanking Julie in his usual charming manner. Julie smiled at me and left, closing the door behind her.

I poured the coffee and handed Jack a cup.

"I had a telephone call from Edna this morning," I said, starting the conversation.

"How is she? Will she be coming back soon?" he questioned.

"No, she won't. That's what she wanted to tell us," I answered. "After discussing the situation of her sister's health with her, they both realise that she will never be well enough to live by herself again, so Edna has decided to retire and live with her sister permanently."

"Oh, that's a shame; it's going to mean quite a change for us."

"Well, I don't know if it will really, especially if Julie will stay with us permanently."

"Do you think she will? It would be great if she would. Are you going to ask her?"

"Yes, I'll do it today, but we need to discuss Edna's pension and I think we should give her some sort of severance pay, don't you?"

"Yes, of course, can I leave that to you to sort out? You're so much better at that sort of thing than I am," he said, looking very sheepish at me.

"If that's OK with you?"

Jack put his cup down on the tray and was about to leave when there was a knock on the door and Charles and Julie entered the room.

"Seeing as you were both together, would you mind if we had a quick word with you?" Julie asked.

"Yes, of course, Julie, do both come in," I replied.

They both came in and I noticed that they were holding hands.

"Charles has asked me to marry him and I have accepted," said Julie, looking up at Charles.

"Oh, how wonderful," I said, getting up and hugging Julie and then shaking hands with Charles. "Congratulations, Charles. I am so pleased for you both."

Jack was now also on his feet congratulating them both but looking somewhat surprised.

"This needs a celebration drink; it's not too early is it?" he said. "No, of course, it isn't. Stay here, I'll get some bubbles."

"Sit down, both of you. I think Jack will insist on celebrating. It's just the sort of good news we need at the moment. Have you thought about the wedding you want?" I asked.

"We just want a quiet wedding without any fuss," said Julie.

"Are you sure?" I asked.

"Yes," said Charles. "We have discussed it and it's what both of us want."

"Well, whatever you want, please let us know what we can do to help," I said.

Jack came back into the room with a bottle of champagne and four glasses. He quickly handed each of us a glass and popped the bottle of bubbly, filling each of our glasses.

"Congratulations again to both of you," he said. "Here's to you, Charles and Julie, all the best for the future."

We all sipped our champagne and whilst Jack spoke to Charles, I pulled Julie to one side and informed her about Edna and asked her if she would like to stay on with us permanently.

She seemed overjoyed and gushed to Charles with the good news.

"You will have to decide where you make your future living quarters, although I think Edna's quarters are the larger and there is access to a second floor which she never used but it is there if you want it. We will look at it tomorrow to see if there is any work and updating that needs to be done. Edna has let me know what items she wants to be sent to her and I have asked Jack's secretary to arrange for that to be done so liaise with her then if you need new furniture we can go and have a shopping spree."

"Oh, thank you, madam, that would be wonderful," said Julie, beaming all over her face. Charles looked happy also and rather flushed from the champagne.

After the small celebration Jack stayed settled on the sofa.

"It's funny isn't it?" he said after a few moments,

"What's that Darling?" I asked.

"We live our lives here involved with all that's happening, forgetting that there are other people living their own lives around us with their own happiness and sadness, beginnings and endings," he said.

I looked over at him, feeling a song starting to be written in his head. He quickly got up and disappeared. I knew he was headed back to the studio with lyrics already forming.

The following morning, Julie, Charles and I had a look at Edna's living quarters. These were beyond the kitchen and overlooked the garden. As with Edna, these were very neat and tidy, with pretty curtains and highly polished furniture. There were already boxes stacked with Edna's belongings ready to ship to her and the furniture she had asked for was marked for shipment.

I didn't remember ever being in here previously, Edna kept to herself and was a private person. The small dining room she had used as her bedroom and the stairs to a first floor had been closed off.

Charles managed to open this door and we found two bedrooms and a large bathroom that had never been used. We all agreed that the ground floor looked fine but this first floor needed redecorating and the bathroom updating. Charles said he would contact a decorator and plumber and let me have the estimates for the work. I left them both looking round and discussing their new home.

I then phoned Amos to see how he was and how the funeral arrangements were progressing.

"I'm OK," he said, although I was not convinced. "I'm keeping busy, which helps I just feel He's going to walk in any moment I still can't believe He's gone. I find it hard to think that the world is still turning and life is carrying on as before."

"I'm so sorry Amos, is there anything I can do to help? Would you like me to come over? I can you know if you want?"

"No, I am being looked after by my lovely sister-in-law and just going through the motions of making the necessary arrangements. I have managed to contact most of our friends. They have all been supportive, although so surprised at the suddenness of his death. The tentative date for the funeral is the 14th, which is just in two weeks' time. The Funeral Directors are making all the arrangements from the list of things I want carried out they seem very efficient."

"I'm glad."

"There is one thing I wanted to ask of you," Amos said quietly.

"Anything I can do to help you, just have to say."

"Will you say something at the service?" he asked.

"Of course I will. I'm so pleased you asked," I said.

"Thank you. It means so much to me. I'll let you know what you will be reading so you can practise beforehand."

"Thank you, Amos, but let me know if there is anything else I can do, I'm here for you."

"Thanks," he replied and then he was gone.

I made a few more calls that needed to be done and when I heard Jack arrive from the studio, I went to join him for lunch.

We had a leisurely lunch and I brought Jack up to date with the morning's news. He informed me that he and the band were starting a new album and over the next few weeks and they would be arriving to work on the arrangements. I realised that I would not be seeing much of him and he would be totalling engrossed in the work being done in the studio.

"That's fine," I told him. "But I expect you to be available for the funeral and if Charles and Julie want us to be involved in the wedding for that too."

"Of course, it goes without saying," he replied. "Do you want to go for a walk later on? I think I will need some fresh air by then. We can take the dogs they enjoy a run in the woods."

"That would be lovely; I shall be around when you are ready."

With that, he left again for the studio and I continued with the catching up I had to do.

Chapter 28

I was discussing supper with Julie when Jack appeared in the kitchen. He already had his coat and walking boots on so I hurried to get ready as patience was not one of his qualities. The dogs were rounded up and we set off along the drive and headed for the vast amount of woodland that surrounded the property. The dogs bounded along, running in front of us but never letting us out of their sight. I am also sure I noticed one of the security men following at a discrete distance behind us and I felt that Stephen's recent appearance had robbed us of even more of our privacy.

We walked arm in arm and I was surprised how chilly it seemed in the wind.

"How's the writing coming along?" I asked.

"Really good," Jack replied. "We have more than enough for a new album but the boys have to review it and make adjustments where they think."

"Does that mean there will be a tour when the album is released?"

"I suppose so," he replied. "But I don't want to do a long time on the road. I shall only agree to a few one night only gigs. Why will you miss me?" he said, pulling me towards me and kissing me.

"Of course, I'll miss you but I was hoping for us to get away for a while and take a long holiday. We always said if we got time we would go back to Australia and really explore the country because last time we were there you were so busy performing here, there and everywhere we never had time to enjoy the place. I think with everything that's been going on, we could do with a long break."

"That sounds like a great idea," Jack replied.

"Do you really mean that?" I said, looking at him straight in the eyes.

"Yes, Yes I do," he said, picking me up and twirling me around whilst laughing.

Jack tripped and we both tumbled to the ground and the dogs came bounding over to us, both thinking we were playing a game and wanting to join in. I was still laughing when Jack stood up and held out his hand to help me up; he was still smiling at me and I was still laughing when I looked up and saw the most dreadful thing I have ever seen. I let out the shrillest of screams, making Jack turn round and look up.

"Oh my God, oh my God," he said it twice, not believing his eyes.

Within seconds, two security men were beside us, one asking what had happened. All I could do was point in the air.

Immediately one of the security men heaved and was violently sick the other was on the phone to presumably Charles.

"Do you know who he is?" the second man asked.

Jack was still standing still, looking up at the body of the man hanging from the tree.

"I think it's Stephen. Oh my God, I think it's Stephen," Jack cried, putting his head in his hands.

Within moments, two vehicles arrived and Charles and two other security men got out of the cars.

"Fuck!" said Charles. "Who is it do we know?"

"Jack seems to think it's Stephen," I said.

When he finished, he turned to Jack and said, "You and Mrs London should go back to the house, I've called the police and if they need to speak to you, they can come to the house."

"No, I'm staying," said Jack. "Can you get one of the security guys to take my wife and the dogs back?"

"Yes, of course, but I think you should go as well," said Charles. "Joe, will you take Mrs London and the dogs back in the car? Make sure she is safe in the house before you come back."

Joe kindly rounded up the dogs and drove us all back to the house. He had a quiet word with Julie on our arrival and left to return to Charles.

I explained to Julie exactly what was happening.

"Are you sure it is Stephan?" she asked.

"Well, Jack does, but to tell you the truth, I could not look too closely. It was just too awful. I think the birds had been pecking at it," I said, shivering as I spoke.

"I'll make some coffee you look frozen," she suggested.

"I think I'll have a brandy with that and pour yourself one, I could do with the company right now."

Julie came back with a pot of coffee and the brandy decanter and two glasses. She sat with me saying very little but I think we were both glad of the company.

The rest of the evening passed very slowly. We heard numerous vehicles go by, some with flashing blue lights, but no one came in to tell us what was happening. After an hour or so, Julie thought she would make sandwiches and flasks of coffee to take up to Jack and Charles and whoever else was there. This she did but before she got the chance to leave, Joe came back to check on us and let us know what was happening.

Evidently, a forensics team had arrived and was busy examining the area. Both Jack and Charles had positively identified Stephen and were waiting in case the police needed any further information. Joe went away with the flasks and the sandwiches, which he assured us would be very welcome.

Julie made me a light supper, after which I said I would go take a bath and get ready for bed but would sit up and wait for Jack to come home. Julie thought she would do the same and sit up, waiting for Charles.

It was just before twelve when Jack came in; He looked as if he had aged 20 years. I poured him a drink and asked if he wanted a hot drink but he just shook his head as if too exhausted to speak. Neither of us spoke and eventually I said, come on, let's go to bed. As soon as his head hit the pillow, he was fast asleep.

The following morning, I was already in the kitchen when Jack came down. He said good morning and kissed me on the cheek.

"I'm sorry about last night," he said to me. "I just couldn't speak anymore I was just so absolutely shattered and the shock was so raw."

"I know, you don't have to apologise. Here, come and have some coffee. I'll make us some breakfast," I offered.

"I'll take the coffee but I don't think I could eat anything at the moment."

"OK, sit here and have coffee and tell me what the police says will happen next."

Chapter 29

He started to speak but his voice and hands were shaking. "There will have to be an inquest but they believe he committed suicide. There was a letter addressed to me in his pocket but I was not allowed to read it, they took it away as evidence."

"I can't believe he did that," I said. "I know he was not quite right in the head but to do this he must have lost it completely."

"The last time he was here he wasn't making any sense," Jack said so quietly I could hardly hear him. "He was rambling on about not knowing what she had done, saying I didn't understand."

"He was acting quite demented, like he had taken something, drugs always reacted badly on his mental state. I paid for him to go to rehab several times and for a while it worked but he always went back he couldn't help himself."

"Yes, he could, Jack," I said. "People do all the time if they really want to."

"I know," Jack said.

Jack pulled me close to him and buried his head in my body I could feel him start to sob and all I could do was hold him till he stopped.

It was Julie coming in to the room that made him move away from me and stand up.

"I'm sorry to disturb you but the police are here and need to speak to Mr Jack," she said.

"Thank you, Julie," I said. "Show them into the sitting room and we will be with them in a moment."

As she left, I asked Jack to go and wash his face and come in when he is ready. Jack nodded his head without saying anything and left the kitchen.

I took a deep breath and went to speak to the police.

"Good morning," I said whilst shaking hands with the two policemen now sitting in the sitting room.

"My husband will be with us in a moment. Can I offer you some tea whilst we wait?" I asked.

By the time the tea arrived and was poured, Jack came into the room and apologised for the delay. He looked composed and more like his usual self.

The police went over the same details over and over again. They confirmed that they had found a note on the body addressed to Jack but did not want us to see it or read it for the moment.

We were also asked about Stephen's wife, Simone, but we knew very little about them as a couple. We couldn't tell the police where they lived or anything about their way of life. The only thing we knew was about her obsession with Jack and her animosity or hatred towards me, which was already documented and in the hands of the police. The two policemen went away, leaving us with no more information that we had before.

On the third day, we had a visit from the detectives that were investigating the death of Stephen.

They looked very dour when they arrived and were shown into the large sitting room where we were waiting for them. Julie offered them tea or coffee to which they both accepted and then she left us to deal with whatever they wanted to ask this time. However, the first detective whose name was Beverley surprised us by saying that they had almost completed their enquires and wanted to bring us up to date with their findings so far.

"Your brother Stephen's death," he began, "has been agreed as a suicide and we have a copy of his suicide note here for you to read. We need to keep the original for the moment. Before we give you that to read, we would like to inform you that on investigating the details given in that note, we were led to a second death."

"A second death?" queried Jack. "Who for God's sake?"

"Stephen's wife Simone, we found her strangled in their apartment. We are led to believe that your brother killed his wife and then took his own life."

"No, I can't believe it," said Jack, "He was very distressed when he came to see me but he never mentioned anything which would have led me to believe he had committed murder. Why would he have killed Simone? He was besotted by her he was totally under her spell."

"It was something he had learnt, something she had told him," Detective Beverley said.

"We believe that she was responsible for the death of Christine London and after taking fingerprints and DNA samples from her body, we discover that she was definitely on the scene in Miss London's flat."

"Oh my God!" I gasped. "After all this time, we find out that she was there."

"Yes," Detective Beverley replied. "The unknown figure prints that we could not identify at the scene of Miss London's death match those taken from Simone."

Both Jack and I sat in silence, not knowing what to say.

He grabbed my hand and held it so tightly it hurt. "Can I read the letter?" he asked.

The second detective handed him a piece of paper and Jack opened it and began to read. I managed to read some of it before he had finished it. By this time, silent tears were running down his cheeks.

He wiped them away with the back of his hand but they still continued to trickle down his cheeks. He was speechless. Detective Beverley got up to leave and held out his hand to Jack to shake. Jack looked at his hand for a few seconds before realising he was meant to shake it but this he did and began to show them out.

"If you need any further information or if we can help in any way here is my card. Please contact us if you need to."

Jack took the card and thanked them both. By the time he came back into the room, I had finished the letter and I too was crying.

"It feels like a chasm has opened up in front of me," Jack said. "And I am falling into it without being able to help myself, even wondering if I want any help."

He came over to me, putting his arms around me and holding on so tightly.

I couldn't say anything to him, my voice wouldn't work. We both just sat there hugging each other and crying. I don't know how long we sat like that but we only drew apart when Jack kissed me on the cheek and said "I love you so much I don't know how I will get through this without you."

"We will get through this together," I said to him. "At least now we know what happened. After all these years of wondering, never knowing what really happened."

"According to Stephen's note, she had been befriending Chrissy for months, trying to get closer to me," Jack said quietly. Chrissy must have twigged eventually and an almighty row ensued. Stephen seemed to think Chrissy's death was an accident but that Simone panicked and tried to make it look like suicide."

"When Stephen found out what she had done," I continued. "He couldn't live with the knowledge she was the one responsible for Chrissy's death. But to do what he did, he just couldn't be in his right mind."

I think we were both totally numb. We spent the rest of the day going through all that we had learnt in a few short hours. We should have felt relief that the nightmare we had been living with for so long was finally over but I don't think we did. Chrissy's death was still raw. Even after all these years, nothing could take away the pain we both felt.

In fact, the knowledge of what had happened brought it all back as if it was yesterday. I still was aware of the pain and horror she must have felt in the last few moments of her life when everybody who loved her couldn't help.

"I need to make some calls," said Jack. "But I think I will wait for tomorrow. I wonder when they will release his body. As much as I hate it, I suppose I will have to arrange the funeral."

"Well, don't expect me to attend. You can leave him to rot wherever he is," I said.

"Darling, I don't think I have ever heard you speak like that before. He was my brother," Jack said quietly, almost under his breath.

"No, he wasn't. Even that was a lie. I know you promised your mother to look after him, but do you think she would have forgiven him for all that he has done? Let's face it, he chose to drink and take drugs till his brain was burnt out. Even after you supporting through two bouts of rehab, he still went straight back to his addictive ways."

He didn't answer and I know he still felt some sort of responsibility for Stephen, more than just loyalty to his mother and the promise that he had made.

So far the story had not hit the papers, but the day of the inquest there were more reporters in attendance that anyone else. I didn't go but Jack had to give evidence so he had to attend.

Charles said it was a nightmare. They had difficulty getting through the crowd of people outside the coroner's court and he had no doubt that Jack would be front-page news tomorrow.

It was in all the newspapers the following day. Not just the inquest, but every aspect of our lives. Chrissy's death, my business, the association with the McKenzie family, Jack and Stephen's childhood, even photos of them as children, where do they get their information from? We expected the story to run for days but fate took a hand that evening there was a private plane crash with a minor member of the Royal family on board and that news took over the front page.

Jack shut himself away and only appeared in the evenings and had very little to say to anyone, including me. He arranged with Charles to cut the security back and, except for a couple of guards at the gate, we recovered some of our privacy.

Jack accompanied me to John Cutler's funeral and, although there were over two hundred and fifty people at the service, we were not an object of interest. Amos looked pale and quite ill but he managed to get through the day, I think he was pleased so many of their friends had turned up and it showed what high esteem people held in both of them.

I spoke to Amos during the afternoon and asked if he wanted to come and stay with us for a while but he declined saying we had enough to cope with at the moment.

"How's Jack?" he asked.

"Oh, you know, Jack, hiding away from the world, not facing reality, but he'll come round when he is ready. He'll go back to writing and performing. What are you going to do with yourself?" I asked.

"Some friends have offered me a beautiful lodge on Loch Lomond and Janine and I are going to stay for a few weeks. She is much more a country girl and is better suited to the outdoors. She has been a rock these last few weeks, she reminds me so much of him."

"I should have been here more for you I'm sorry," I said.

"No, don't be, you are a true friend. In all honesty, I don't think anything could have helped me. I miss him so much."

"I'm so sorry, Amos," We hugged each other for a few minutes and when we drew apart, there were tears in his eyes.

"Come, I must go back to my guests," he said.

Jack and I left soon afterwards. He was silent for some time in the car when he suddenly turned to me and grabbed my hand. "I'm sorry," he said. "I will try to be more communicative. At the moment, I just feel so lost."

"It's OK, I understand. Just know I am here when you are ready," I said to him, kissing him on the cheek.

"Thank you," he replied and said no more than that.

We made love that night and in the morning we actually sat down to breakfast together. He even asked Julie how the wedding plans were progressing. She seemed a little taken back but replied everything was about sorted and going quite well.

"Good, Charles has asked me to be his best man," he said, quite out of the blue.

"Has he?" I queried.

"Yes," he said. "That's OK isn't it?"

"Of course that's great," I said.

Jack got to his feet, kissed me and disappeared.

Julie and I looked at each puzzled but made no comment.

Chapter 30

"Now Julie, stop what you're doing and tell me all about the arrangements for the wedding. I want to know if there is anything I can do to help," I asked.

"Well, everything is arranged, I think. The church, the choir, flowers, I have to speak to the caterers this morning to confirm the numbers and how many vegetarians to cater for. My dress is here, I had the final fitting last week and as long as I eat nothing from now until the day of the wedding, it will fit beautifully," she said laughing slightly nervously.

"You seem to have everything sorted," I said, smiling. "What about the honeymoon? Where are you planning to go?" I asked.

"Well, we have decided not to go away; we most probably will spend the night in the hotel. If I have to tell you the truth, Mrs London, we have spent our money on the tickets for my daughter and her husband to come over from Australia because I wanted her to be at my wedding. She's the only family I have and I think it's important she meets Charles. We both wanted them both to be here."

"My goodness," I exclaimed. "All this time I have known you and I never knew you had a daughter. How absolutely wonderful. Of course, you would want her at your wedding."

"She's married to an Australian she met whilst back packing during her gap year from university. I have only managed to get out there once to visit her and I miss her terribly. I'm as excited to be seeing her again as I am to be getting married. Does that sound selfish?" she asked.

"Of course not," I said. "I'm looking forward to meeting her now I know that she exists. Also, it gives me an idea for a wedding present for you and Charles. What would you say to a fortnight at the house in the Algarve, all expenses paid? You have been there before and know what it's like. What do you say?"

"Oh, it sounds wonderful. I'll have to discuss it with Charles, but I'm sure he will love the idea. But can you spare us both?"

"Of course, we can. I may even be able to cook a few meals whilst you are away, though not to your standard, of course," I said, smiling.

It was lunchtime before I saw Jack again.

"Wills has been on the phone," he said as he came in. "I've invited him and Emily for lunch on Sunday. They asked if they could bring Logan with them. That's OK isn't it?"

"Yes, of course, it is," I replied. "It will be nice to see them all. Actually, I wanted to run something by you that concerns Wills and Emily."

"OK, what are you cooking up now?" he said, pulling me close to him and kissing me.

"It's about the flat at Chelsea Harbour," I said.

"Gosh, forgotten all about that. When was the last time we used it?"

"Well, that's what brought it to mind. I know Wills and Emily are planning to have a house built in Surrey but with Wills working all sorts of long shifts at St Thomas's the flat would be an ideal London base for them and since we haven't thought about a wedding present for them, I would like to give them the flat. What do you say?"

"Of course, it's a wonderful gesture but I'm not contributing in any way. What can I give to help?" he asked, sounding disappointed.

"Well, it will need a refurb so perhaps you can offer to cover those costs and whatever else they want to make it the way they want it," I suggested.

"Thanks, I do love you so you know and I don't mind being part of any plans you have, you know that, don't you?" he said, pulling me towards him and kissing me hard.

Well, like you say we don't use it and it would be so useful to Wills. That is, of course, if they want it and whilst we are on the subject of giving things away, I have offered Charles and Julie the Portugal villa for their honeymoon. I hope that's OK with you?"

"Of course, it is. Does that mean I get you all to myself for two weeks?" he asked, still holding onto me tighter than ever.

"Oh yes, me and my cooking."

"Well, it's not the best thing you do but I can put up with that. I better sort out some take away menus," he said, laughing.

I hit him lightly on the shoulder, pretending to feel indignant.

"You make everything turn out so perfectly; I don't know what I would do without you. What can I do for you? There must be something you would like?"

"What about that holiday we talked about? We deserve some time for ourselves. Why don't you think about organising that?"

"You know I think I will," he said smiling and kissing me again we went into have lunch laughing and holding each other.

Chapter 31

Sunday lunch was a real family affair, with dad joining for the day. I was a little concerned about him, he suddenly seemed old and frail, but he assured me he was fine and enjoyed playing with little Logan. Wills and Emily were so surprised at being offered the Chelsea Harbour property as it seemed to answer all their prayers. Emily had already found a preschool for Logan near to the hospital and they had already started to look at properties to rent.

We arranged to meet at Chelsea Harbour in the week so that Wills and Emily could look at the apartment and discuss what improvements were needed to make the property into a family friendly home.

I had heard from Amos and he was settled in the Scottish Highlands and was enjoying the solitary environment with his sister-in-law. They were walking and doing some sightseeing and there was some discussion about climbing Ben Nevis! He made me smile but at least he was keeping busy and seemed content.

Julie's daughter was due to arrive on Tuesday morning and Julie said that she and her husband could not believe they would be staying in a rock star's home. Julie said they were both fans and it seemed to be as exciting as coming to England and attending the wedding.

I asked dad to stay the night but he insisted on going home which was a mistake on my part as the following morning I had a call from the warden of the complex where he lived to say she had called the doctor as he had a bit of a turn in the night.

I arranged to go over when the doctor was due. I asked Julie to make sure the spare room was ready because I would be bringing him home regardless of his prostrations. Jack asked if I needed him to come with me but I said no, which I think he was pleased about as he had Robin and his manager, arriving during the morning but I did need Charles to help me if dad was to come back with me. I told Charles I was sorry to be taking him away from all the wedding arrangements but I have a feeling he welcomed the intrusion.

We arrived a little while before the doctor and I was upset at the way dad looked. He was very pale and seemed unable to speak or focus on what was going on around him. When the doctor arrived and gave him a thorough examination, he confirmed my worst fears, dad had had a stroke. Dr Simpson wanted dad to go to hospital for some tests but said I most probably could take him home after that. I explained to dad what was happening and although he was a little frightened; he said as long as I stayed with him, he was OK.

It was after 9 o'clock at night before we arrived back home but the nurse I had managed to engage during the day was there to greet us. She was a rather large coloured lady with the most engaging smile and was called Honey Simpson. Dad took to her right away as she fused over him something rotten.

"Now you call me Honey Daddy and we will get on just fine," she said in a rather loud voice. I was about to say that dad's hearing was fine, but he smiled at her and said, "Thank you." So I left them to get acquainted and said I would be up to see him as soon as he was settled.

"Thank you for all your help Charles I'll let you have a quieter day tomorrow," I said to Charles as we entered the house.

"You're welcome I'm only too pleased to help," he replied.

Jack was waiting in the sitting room for me and as soon as I entered the room, he handed me a large drink, which I gulped at before sitting down.

"You look absolutely wacked," he said. "How is he?"

"Well, the doctor says it seems to have been a minor stroke and hopefully he will make a good recovery. They've put him on some medication and they will keep an eye on him with follow-up appointments for him but at the moment he is to rest and take care."

"Sorry, Darling, I haven't been much help to you today," Jack said, kissing me on the top of my head and taking my glass off me to refill.

"It's OK, there wasn't much you could have done but tomorrow we need some time to sit and discuss things if it's alright with you. We seem to have been passing each other without connecting just lately. Don't pour anymore in that glass as I haven't eaten anything today and that has gone straight to my head," I replied.

Just then there was a knock and Julie brought a tray of soup and cold meats and salad in.

"Charles told me you hadn't eaten all day so I thought you may like this," she said.

"Oh, thank you, Julie, you are a lifesaver."

When I finished eating, I went up to see dad. Honey met me at his door and said he had just nodded off so I left her and said we would speak tomorrow about his future ongoing care. With that I went to bed and I too was asleep as soon as my head touched the pillow.

The following morning I woke to a grey day with rain falling and it seemed I felt the same as the day looked. I went down to breakfast to find that Jack was already up and in the studio. Julie told me he would see me at eleven for coffee and would then be mine for the rest of the day.

As soon as I had breakfast, I went to see dad. He looked as if he had a little more colour and was actually laughing with Honey. I could see she was going to be good for Him. Honey and I sat and talked about her duties and what I expected from her but she already had prepared a treatment plan and some light exercise. So after some chat with dad I was happy to leave him in Honey's careful hands. Honey wanted him to stay in bed for a couple of days before he got up and joined the rest of us so I asked her to liaise with Julie about his dietary needs.

The next hour was spent with Julie, discussing her absence during her honeymoon and what plans she had put in place for the smooth running of the house. I had hoped that Jack and I would be able to get a few days away but with dad being with us, this would now not be possible.

"I've arranged for Hilary to take over from me. She has become a reasonably good cook and she has been with us for a number of years now so she knows the running of the house quite well," Julie informed me.

"Which one is Hilary?" I asked.

"She's one of the daily girls that comes in, the one that's engaged to Dale, our gardener," she replied.

"Oh yes, I know she was telling me they are saving up for a flat so they can get married, although I don't think they are having much luck," I said.

"Yes, that's her. She's very pleasant and quite bright as a hard worker. In fact, I have a suggestion to put to you with regards to that and I hope I'm not speaking out of turn," she said, with a little query in her voice.

"I'm sure whatever you have to say will be more than welcome," I replied.

"Well, now that Charles and I are completely moved into our new quarters and the flat is free over the garages. I thought it might be a good idea to have Dale and Hilary living here on the premises and that flat would be more than suitable for a young couple starting out in married life. It could be very useful as a cover to have Hilary on the premises."

"I think that's a wonderful idea. You are so cleaver Julie. Would you like to discuss it with them? Do you have the time before you go away?" I asked.

"I would love to. Shall I speak to the solicitors to get some documents drawn up?" she asked.

"Yes, please, if they could get it all done prior to you going away, that would be lovely. If the flat needs any repair or decoration we will, of course, pay for that if they can just let me have some quotes that would be great. Now, is there anything else we need to discuss?" I asked.

"There's just one thing I would like to ask of you."

"Yes, what is it?" I asked.

"Whilst we are away on honeymoon, my daughter and son-in-law intend to travel and do some sightseeing. When we come back home, I would like them to finish their holiday here with us. It would be for two weeks and I just want to make sure that's OK with you?"

"Yes, of course, it is. You can have whomever you like to stay in your home, Julie."

"Thank you," Julie said, standing to leave. "I'll let you know how I get on with Hilary and Dale."

Chapter 32

The next few days went by in a blur. Hilary and Dale were delighted to be offered the flat above the garages previously occupied by Charles. There seemed to be little to do to it, as Charles had kept it in a pretty decent condition.

Every time I saw either of them, they couldn't stop thanking both Jack and myself. I offered to take both of them through the attics to look through the furniture that was stored there. They were delighted and picked several pieces. I think money was tight and it helped them set up their new home so that any money they had could be used on planning their wedding day.

"Are you sure you don't mind us having this furniture?" they asked.

"Of course, that's the reason it's up here because it's surplus to requirements. Help yourself to anything you need," I said and left them sorting through the furniture.

We met Wills and Emily at Chelsea Harbour and they felt the apartment was just right for both of them. It was close to the hospital for Wills and very near to the schools they had picked out for Logan. They both still wanted a house in the country as a weekend bolt hole but I think Emily was a city girl at heart and Chelsea really suited her. Jack and I left them discussing plans to turn the staff quarters into a nursery wing whilst he whisked me off to the Ritz for a champagne lunch.

Dad continued to improve albeit very slowly, but a physiotherapist was employed to help Honey with his treatment and dad was determined to make progress as he did not like to be so inactive.

Julie and Charles were busy finalising their wedding plans and Julie, Hilary and I met to discuss the work and management of the household whilst Julie took time off and was away on honeymoon. Hilary seemed a very sensible girl and took her duties very seriously. She had started preparing our evening meals and they were very good, Jack loved her rather heavy puddings and I thought if he kept on eating the second helpings he was being offered, he would have a problem with his weight.

The funeral took place of Stephen. I did not attend, although I believe some of the tour support people did attend and some members of the band were also there. He was buried by his father. Jack was quite all the rest of that day but he said he was glad it was all over.

Julie's daughter and son-in-law arrived, much to Julie's delight. We only had time to be introduced to Susan and Eddie as they were exhausted with travelling but Jack and Julie were going to give them a tour of the property the following day when they had rested and the next evening Jack and I arranged to take them all out to a local restaurant as a pre wedding meal to celebrate their arrival.

Susan was a tall heavy-set woman who obviously was a fan of Jacks. She hardly noticed me but giggled and smiled at Jack like a school girl but I was used to that sort of behaviour. She spoke with a slight Australian accent, unlike her husband who had a strong accent. They both were tanned but Eddie had a swarthy look and I guessed he worked out of doors. I liked him straight away; he had a twinkle in his eyes and his smile put you at ease.

I was sat in the garden the following morning with my second cup of coffee when I saw Eddie coming towards me lighting a cigarette.

"Hello there," I shouted. "Have you had enough of the tour and the Jack London appreciation club?"

"I'm sorry," he said, smiling. "I like his music but I can't say I'm a real fan and I needed a ciggie, Julie says you don't like smoking in the house."

"No, she's right, I'm sorry," I said.

"That's alright I'd rather be outside."

I asked him to sit beside me and he did.

"You've a lovely garden here," he said. "I believe Jack said that was your domain?"

"Yes, it's my love and the way I relax, although I can't take all the credit, I do have an army of gardeners doing all the heavy work and the day-to-day stuff. What do you do for a living back home?"

"Well, my official title is landscape gardener but in reality I'm one of that army of gardeners that you have here."

"Do you enjoy it?" I asked.

"Absolutely love it," he replied. "I'm basically my own boss, I'm outdoors all day and my clients appreciate the work I do. Although we don't have gardens like this back in Sidney, I suppose you would call them more arid gardens."

"Well, that certainly wouldn't work here," I said, smiling. "Would you like to meet my head gardener, he's a lovely chap? He's currently completing a flower garden for me so I have cut flowers all year round."

"I've noticed the flower arrangements around the house. Are they down to you?"

"Yes, another hobby. Come on, let's go and find Dale."

We walked around the house stopping each time something caught Eddie's eye and he asked questions about which plants we had used. I introduced him to Dale when we finally reached him and they were immediately engrossed in types of soil and the drainage of the patch Dale was currently working on. I slipped away, feeling very unwanted.

That evening at the restaurant, everything went very well. Julie was happy to have her daughter with her. Charles was happy because Julie was. Eddie was enthusiastic about meeting Dale and the garden. Susan was hanging on every word Jack spoke and I was happy to see everyone else so happy. It was a very successful night.

I overslept the next morning, the day of the wedding. I'm no longer use to late nights and I am sure I drank too much red wine.

"Wakey, wakey," I heard Jack call as I roused myself from slumber.

"My gosh! What time is it?" I asked, rubbing my eyes.

"It's nearly nine and if you don't get a move on, we will be late for this wedding," Jack said. "Here's a cup of coffee for you."

"Thanks," I said, taking a gulp of coffee and getting out of bed at the same time. "I'll jump in the shower."

When I came out of the shower, Jack was dressed and sat reading the paper whilst drinking another coffee.

"How come you are up and ready and so cheerful?" I asked.

"Best man," he said. "I take my duties very seriously."

"Since when?" I said, smiling. "I don't think you have ever taken anything seriously in your life."

"I'm turning over a new leaf," he said jokingly. "Now get a move on."

"Have you seen my little Channel watch?" I asked. "You know, the one with the little black strap."

"You leave that watch all over the place. We found it in the fridge once."

"I'm sure I left it here," I said, opening and shutting all the drawers of the dressing table.

"Oh, come on, wear one of the others, you have plenty."

It was a lovely wedding. The sun shone and everything went off without a hitch. Julie looked beautiful and Charles seemed so proud to be by her side.

The reception was lovely, Julie had themed the colours so well and matched her bouquet with Charles' tie and waistcoat. Jack's speech was so funny without being too rude, everyone laughed.

There was a local band which went on playing well into the night and Jack and I danced as much as we could together when Susan allowed him some time with me. She seemed to be besotted with him and I had to remind him that he had only just got over one stalker and we did not need another.

It started to be a little game between us. How long we could spend together before she interrupted us? Later during the evening, I overheard Eddie telling her to stop making a fool of herself.

It was a late night again and needless to say I slept in again. After breakfast, I went to see dad and tell him about the day and all that had happened at the wedding. I could hear people talking below the window and when I looked out there were Dale and Eddie digging over a patch of garden and chatting away like pals that had known each other all their lives. They were certainly getting on together. I wondered how Susan was occupying herself and I hoped she was with her mother, helping her to pack and get ready for her honeymoon.

However, when I met Jack at lunch, I discovered she had spent the morning in the studio with him watching and listening to him work. He decided to spend the afternoon with me out of her way, which was nice for me but I thought her attentions were becoming a bit too intrusive for Jack.

Jack left early the next morning. He would be away a few days with his Agent, his music producer and some of the band. They had been working on a new album and I presumed that would mean another tour in the planning.

As I walked into the kitchen, Hilary was there cooking something at the stove that smelt lovely.

"I thought I would cook you pancakes for breakfast as a treat," she said, smiling. "You do like them, don't you?" she asked.

"They are my absolute favourite, Hilary," I answered. "I think you must be on a mission to fatten Jack and myself up and I think it seems to be working."

We both laughed. Breakfast was great. There was fresh coffee, blue berries and yogurt for the pancakes, which Hilary had to help me eat as there was quite a mountain of them.

"I thought I would give the master bedroom a good going over this morning and look for the missing watch whilst I was doing it," Hilary said.

"Oh, thank you, Hilary. I can't imagine what I've done with it. I'm also missing a pair of sapphire earrings if you come across them when you're up there," I informed her. "I seem to be losing things right, left and centre."

"Don't worry; I'm sure they will turn up."

"Thanks, Hilary," I said, pouring another cup of coffee.

I spent the rest of the morning catching up on correspondence and telephone calls and when I finished, I went upstairs to see how Hilary was getting on. The bedroom was in complete disarray.

"Hello, madam," she said as I entered the room. "Well, I can safely say there is no watch or earrings in this room. I have looked everywhere."

"I can see you have," I said, looking around. "You seem to have been very thorough."

We both started laughing.

"I'll soon have everything back to normal."

"Let's forget it for the moment I'm sure they will turn up," I said.

I was about to leave when Susan turned up at the door of the room.

"Susan, what are you doing here?" I asked, rather surprised to see her.

"Oh Hi, I was looking for Jack. Is he here?" she asked, peering into the room.

"No," I said quite bluntly. "Can I help you?"

"I shouldn't think so. He said I was always welcome to watch him working," she replied.

"He would hardly be working up here in the bedroom. I'll walk you back to your mom's quarters."

I walked her back through the house to the kitchen and opened the connecting door to her mother's apartments.

"I would appreciate in future that you did not come into the main house unless accompanied by either Jack or myself, we do value our privacy," I said holding the door open for her.

"Oh, it's OK, Jack doesn't mind," she said with a slight smirk on her face.

"But I do," I replied.

By then, Hilary came into the kitchen.

On closing the door, I turned the key in the lock and put the bolt across the top of the door.

"Until Julie comes home, I think we will keep this door locked and also the front door," I informed Hilary. "I like to know who is in the house."

"Yes, Mrs London," Hilary said. "I'll make sure that the French windows are locked as well."

"Thank you."

Chapter 33

When Jack phoned that evening, I told him about the conversation I had had with Susie and my subsequent decision to lock the connecting door. He was surprised about Susie's attitude, as he could not remember inviting her to watch him working. He suggested I speak to Eddie and sound him out about her behaviour and see if he could have a word with her about 'boundaries'. I did not want to make a big issue about it but if I saw him tomorrow, I may speak to him but I would just test the water first.

"I'm really missing you," he said after a short while.

"You haven't been gone a day yet," I said, smiling to myself.

"I know, but I still miss you. Why don't you come and join me I have a lovely suite here at the Savoy and it's much too big for me. I'm busy in the day but you could do some shopping, catch up with friends and we could have our evenings together and our nights,"

"You're incorrigible, but I have dad to think about."

"Oh, come on, he's got plenty to fuss over him and we won't be too far away if you are needed. Please say you will come and join me."

"Well, I wouldn't mind the break. I'll speak to dad and if he is alright about it, I'll come up tomorrow afternoon."

I spoke to dad after breakfast the following morning and he didn't mind he said I could do with a break and he was well looked after. Hilary said it would be a good opportunity to give the kitchen and main rooms a good clean whilst everyone was out of the way. So I packed a case for a few days and was on my way after lunch.

I did, however, manage to have a few words with Eddie before I left, which was quite enlightening. He apologised for Susie but admitted she had had problems before and became obsessional very quickly with people. He told me she was bipolar and was as right as reign when she took her medication but he had felt just lately she had been behaving a little oddly and wondered if she had come off her medication.

I explained that because of my work I understood about her condition and if he needed any help to let me know.

He thanked me but said he was used to Susie now and he thought he could cope.

I left him to speak to Susie and thought it was most probably a good thing that both Jack and I were away for a few days.

It seemed like ages since I had been up to London and at first it seemed like a strange, unfamiliar place but sitting in the taxi in traffic with the noise all around me I soon remembered the buzz I got from being in the midst of the life London offered. It was better today because I was here to enjoy myself, not to work.

The Savoy was lovely and Jack had booked himself in to a very expensive suite. He always preferred staying in a hotel rather than the flat in Chelsea. I think he secretly liked being waited on, his every whim delivered to him just for the asking. The suite came with a butler so I had nothing to do not even unpack so I booked dinner in our room and decided to have a leisurely bath and await Jack's arrival. I did ask our butler to ensure the front desk did not let anyone know we were in residence if anyone asked.

Jack arrived back about 6 o'clock and seemed really pleased to see me he never did like to be by himself. He showered and changed, then we had drinks and an early dinner. We relaxed in front of the television sipping champagne and brandy eventually going early to bed a little bit squiffy and had the most fabulous drunken sex.

The following morning, I awoke to the smell of freshly brewed coffee.

"I ordered breakfast for us, hope that was OK?" Jack said, kissing me and chewing toast at the same time.

"That's lovely," I said. "I'm famished."

"You always are after a night of passion like last night. I have to say it was wonderful. I am so glad you decided to join me. What are you going to do today?"

"I've arranged to meet Emily for lunch," I replied. "It will be nice to catch up."

"That sounds great," he said, devouring a large English breakfast. "I suppose there will be shopping involved sometime today."

"But of course, it only seems proper, there's so much I need."

"I'm sure you do," Jack said, smiling. "Why don't you see if you can get tickets for a show tonight and we will paint the town. It will be nice to be out together by ourselves for a change?

"OK, I would like that."

We finished breakfast and Jack quickly left, whilst I had time at leisure to read the papers and get ready to do a bit of shopping before meeting Emily back at the hotel for lunch.

I only had time to do a thorough trawl through Selfridges and was laden down with bags on my return to the hotel. Emily arrived soon after and we had a lovely lunch and we chatted non-stop. I caught up with all the alterations that were going on in the Chelsea flat. The servant's quarter was being turned into a nursery and the kitchen was being ripped out and all new appliances being installed. I quickly realised I had been neglecting it for some time and was glad it was being lived in again.

On returning from the lady's room before our sweet was served, I noticed that there was someone I recognised in the foyer. It was Susie. She had been to the desk and was now having a good look around before heading towards the door and leaving. I called one of the waiters over and asked if he could find out for me if she was enquiring for us at the desk.

He returned soon afterwards to our table and said, yes, the young woman had been asking if Mr Jack London was staying in the hotel. She had, of course, been met with a negative. I thanked the waiter and explained to Emily what was going on.

"I can't believe she's here in London trying to track Jack down," I said to Emily. "We just don't seem to get away from these obsessional fans. It's a nightmare."

"You don't think she's dangerous, do you?" Emily asked.

"I hope not," I replied. "I will give her husband a call after lunch and see if he knows what she is up too."

It was late in the afternoon when I managed to phone home and speak to Eddie. He explained that he and Susie had had a terrible row that morning, mostly about her bizarre behaviour towards Jack. He did not realise that Susie had followed us up to London and was really concerned about her.

We spoke for some time and I gave him the telephone number of a colleague at one of the London clinics and I said if Susie became unmanageable to contact him for help. I spoke to my colleague and said he may get a phone call and I explained what was happening.

When Jack arrived back, I told him what had happened and he said he could not believe this was happening again. We both agreed there was little we could do about it whilst away from home but we both felt glad that within the next few days Julie and Charles would be back home and hoped they would be able to sort Susie out. In the meantime, we would stay here in London and keep away from Susie.

We went out to the theatre and afterwards had a late supper at one of Jack's favourite restaurants. For a small time we forgot about Susie and just enjoyed being together.

The following day I went with Jack to the studio and he finished early so we had lunch together and then called at the Chelsea flat to meet Emily and Wills before going back to the hotel with them for an early supper. The following day we were going home as Julie and Charles were due back and we wanted to be there to greet them. In the end we were late leaving as Jack had some last-minute things to finalise and by the time we left it meant we did not get back until late evening and it was quite dark when we arrived.

Hilary met us and after sorting out our bags, had coffee and a light supper sorted out for us. I said thank you and told her she was a blessing it was nice to be home again and I could see she had been hard at work as everything looked wonderful. She said she was sorry that the curtains in the main sitting room had not been rehung but the dry cleaners had let her down and they would not be ready until tomorrow.

"Well, if that's all we have to deal with, I'm sure I'm quite happy," I said to her.

"Charles and Julie are back," Hilary informed us. "They seem to have had a marvellous time and they look so well."

"We were hoping to be back before they arrived home but were delayed," I said. "It's late now but we will catch up tomorrow."

"Thanks, Mrs London, I will just clear away and be off."

"Don't worry," I replied. "I'll clear these things away, you get home and I'll see you in the morning."

Chapter 34

I awoke to Jack kissing me and saying he was in a hurry to get into the studio but should be finished by lunchtime and asked if we could spend the afternoon together. I replied very sleepily that that would be lovely and he quickly disappeared but by then I was quite awake and decided to get up and shower and get ready to meet the day.

It was Julie, making breakfast in the kitchen when I entered.

"Hello, Julie, it's nice to see you back," I said on seeing her. "You have a lovely colour. Did you have a good time and feel suitably relaxed to face the world of Jack London and myself?"

"We had a wonderful time and I thank you for everything you did to make our honeymoon so special," she replied with a smile that beamed from ear to ear.

"I'm so glad," I said. "You both deserved a break you work so hard for us both."

"There is smoked salmon and scrambled eggs for breakfast. Jack has already eaten," she said. "Shall I pour the coffee? If you have time this morning, Eddie and I would like to speak to you about Susie, I understand she has been behaving strangely since we have been away."

"Yes, I'm sorry you have come back to problems but I have been concerned," I replied. "I'm free as soon as breakfast is over."

"We also need to speak about the future rota with yourself and Hilary, she's done very well whilst you have been away."

"Yes, we have already spoken and have some idea about the way forward, if you are in agreement," she said whilst serving me breakfast. "I'll speak to Eddie and perhaps meet at 10 o'clock."

"That's fine," I said. "By the way, this breakfast is delicious."

The meeting later with Eddie, Julia and Charles was very difficult, I could see that Julie was very distressed and she kept apologising for us being involved in her daughter's obsession. It appeared that Susie had had several of these episodes before and mainly happened when she came off her medication.

Susie had assured Eddie and her mother that she was taking her medication, but both believed this was not true. Eddie handed me an envelope and told me he had found the items in Susie's belongings. In the envelope was my little black watch, some of my earrings and several other items I had not even missed. Eddie said that Susie said Jack had given her the items as gifts, which, of course, none of us believed was true.

I explained that I could arrange for Susie to get some help in one of the clinics but it would be better if she volunteered to go in of her own accord, if not it would mean two doctors sectioning her and it could not be me as I knew her. I could see they were all distressed about the situation but in the end they decided to speak to Susie and convince her to get some help voluntarily and if she didn't, they would speak to me again.

After they went away, I telephoned one of the clinics and made them aware of the situation. They agreed to make a room available and waited for my phone call when a decision was made.

In the end, Susie would not voluntarily go into the clinic and became quite violent, eventually locking herself in the bathroom. I called the clinic again and one of the doctors and two of the nurses came to the house. Julie managed to talk Susie out of the bathroom. Colin, the young doctor, spoke to her and gave her some tranquillisers and Susie went quite peacefully to the clinic. Eddie went with them.

The house was suddenly quiet but Julie was obviously very distressed by the whole episode so I told her to go and relax with Charles as I was quite happy to cope on my own and not to worry about anything.

Jack had purposely kept out of the way, knowing that seeing him would only distress Susie even more than she already was. When everything settled, we decided to order in and just relax by the fire together.

"What will happen to her?" Jack asked.

"They will assess her and if they can get her back on her medication, she should quickly respond to treatment, they will keep her closely monitored and just see how she responds. They usually ask relatives to keep away for a short while," I replied. "She is in the best place for her sake and own good and from what I have been told, she has gone through this sort of thing a few times before so she knows the routine."

"I feel sorry for Julie and Eddie, it must be very difficult dealing with this sort of illness," said Jack.

"Yes," I responded. "It certainly is."

Chapter 35

The house went back to the normal routine and we had daily updates on how well Susie was doing and although she was anxious to be home as she told everyone 'Jack needed her' the doctors treating her thought it was going to be a long time before she was back on an even keel. This particular obsessional episode seemed to be deep-rooted and had been coming on for some time.

Susie had been in the clinic for four weeks before she was allowed visitors and Eddie and Julie both went to see her. They each reported that she seemed fine, although she was still anxious to hear about Jack and if he was asking about her. Julie was particularly distressed about her on return from seeing her and asked me if I thought she would ever be well again.

Unfortunately, I could not comment as I was deliberately keeping my distance from Susie's treatment but I did know one of her doctor's had concerns about her.

Jack had finished his current workload and we both felt it would be nice to get away for a few days so we booked flights and went away to the house in Portugal. The weather was good for the time of year and we both enjoyed each other's company. Jack slept well and when we finally came home, he looked so much better.

The morning following our return, I was meeting with both Julie and Hilary to discuss the refurbishment of the guest bedrooms; something that had been planned for quite some time now and eventually the decorator was free from other commitments for the work to commence.

There was a knock on the door and before I could say come in, Charles burst into the room.

"I'm sorry to disturb you," he said breathlessly. "Julie, have you moved my gun for any reason?"

"Your gun?" Julie answered incredulously. "Why would I move your gun? You keep it locked in your gun cupboard."

"I've just gone to the cupboard to check it and clean it and it's missing," Charles answered and was looking quite distressed. "I haven't seen it since we came back from honeymoon. I checked it then but not since. There has been no one else in the apartment except Susie and Eddie and I have already spoken to him."

"If you will excuse me, madam?" Julie said, rising and leaving the table. "You can't be looking properly, Charles. I'll come with you. It must be in the right place."

"Well, I assure you it isn't," Charles said quite sharply following Julie out through the door.

Hilary and I looked at each other and smiled.

"Men can never find anything even when it's right under their noses," Hilary said.

We continued with our discussion when a few moments later, we were interrupted by the telephone. Hilary got up to answer it. After a few moments she said, "It's for you, madam, a Doctor Jameson from the clinic."

"Thank you, Hilary," I said, taking the phone from her. "Hi Tom, how can I help you?"

I listened intently as he informed me that Susie had gone missing and had not been seen since last night. She had last been seen in her room at bedtime but was not there this morning and after an extensive search, could not be found in the facility at all. He said of late she had been getting more and more anxious about Jack and he could only think that she was making her way back to us. He informed me that he had let the police know as he considered her to be a danger both to herself and maybe others. I thanked him for letting me know and put the phone down.

At that moment, Julie followed by Charles came back into the room.

"Well, we have searched everywhere and it has definitely gone," said Julie. "I can't imagine where to."

"I'm sorry, madam, but Charles thinks we should inform the police as it's quite a serious matter," said Julie quite distressed.

"That's quite alright, Julie. Charles, you must do as you think is correct but unfortunately I have some other bad news for you both. I've just heard from the clinic," I said. "Susie has gone missing. Is it possible she has been in the house in the night or this morning?"

"No," said Charles. "We would have known, wouldn't we?"

We all fell silent for a second and the quiet was broken by myself as I shouted, "Jack, where's Jack?"

I started to run from the room, rushing towards the studio and was aware that the others were following me just as quickly. I was just a few yards from the studio door when a noise so terrifying resonated throughout the house. "No, Oh No," I screamed. When a second shot rang out.

The studio door was locked and it took several seconds, although it seemed like forever for Charles to break it down. The sight that greeted us all, I shall never forget. Susie, gun still in hand, lay just inside the door; the top of her head seemed to be missing and there was blood and brain matter on the wall behind her.

There was so much blood everywhere. Julie rushed to her and was screaming and crying. I couldn't see Jack at first but then noticed him on the floor by the console table he too had a bloody wound to his head. I could hear someone screaming and then realised it was me. I cradled Jack's head in my arms and unexpectedly heard him make a sound.

"He's not dead," I shouted. "He's not dead. Hilary, phone the ambulance."

I could see she was already on the phone. I kept rocking Jack in my arms, telling him it was going to be alright. The rest of the time went in a blur. The house was suddenly filled with paramedics, ambulance men and policemen. I went in the ambulance with Jack and waited for what seemed like forever before anyone came to speak to me to let me know what was going on.

Whilst waiting, Wills arrived. I don't know who called him but I was so grateful to see him. After speaking to me for a few minutes, he went away to see if he could find out what was going on. He came back after some time and told me Jack was alive but a bullet was lodged in the temporal part of his skull and he was being taken down to the theatre immediately.

Wills knew the surgeon that was to operate on Jack and told me he was a good surgeon and Jack was in the best possible hands. The surgery took hours but eventually, the surgeon, looking extremely tired, came to speak to us. We were told that the bullet had been removed successfully and although no major damage had been done, it was suspected that Jack had suffered a stroke and it would be sometime before they could assess any damage that might have been caused.

I asked if I could see him and was told yes but not to expect too much, as it was too early to be sure all was well. At that moment, all I could think about was that Jack was still alive and that was all that mattered.

Chapter 36

During the next few days, people came and went as I sat beside Jack. I was told he had been put in an induced coma to help him heal. Police came to interview me but I think I was incoherent and they couldn't make any sense of anything I was telling them. They eventually went away and said they would come back when I was feeling better. Hilary brought me some clean clothes and toiletries whilst I remained by Jack.

She tried to tell me what had happened at home but I couldn't make any sense of what she was saying, so she told me not to worry as everything was being dealt with.

It was ten days before the doctors brought Jack out of his coma and the worst I expected became apparent. Jack's speech had gone and the left side of his body was very week and there was little movement in his limbs. The stroke he had suffered had left him this way.

We both sat there whilst the doctors carried out so many tests and then listened to the prognosis.

They seemed quite upbeat about Jack regaining his strength and speech, which seemed to help Jack understand what was in front of him. In the next few days, they would arrange for Jack to be moved to a private facility to start a regime of physical and mental physiotherapy. The doctors did not mince their words and informed Jack he would have a hard road in front of him and there would be setbacks along the way but there was no reason that he could make a good recovery.

I asked if this could be done at home but it was felt initially that this would be better under hospital supervision until his physical health improved. So after a further four days in hospital Jack was duly transported off to a private rehabilitation hospital and after making sure he was comfortably settled in, I went home.

It seemed so strange to be back, everything the same, but I knew everything was different. Julie was still off work, which is understandable. Hilary was keeping the house running as normally as possible, the studios still had a police presence and they asked if I would talk to them tomorrow.

Charles came to speak to me in the evening and brought me up to date but I stopped going into too much detail, it still was all too much to assimilate.

"I still think it was my fault," he said quietly.

"But why?" I asked. "None of us could have known just how ill Suzie had become."

"It was my gun," he said, "and we had brought her here. Julie is devastated by what Suzie did. I don't think she will ever get over it."

"I'll come and speak to her tomorrow if you think it may help?" I asked.

"Thank you, mam. She needs to know that both you and Jack will be OK."

"I'm sure we will, I hope we will," I answered, feeling like I should have my fingers crossed when saying it.

Chapter 37

Julie looked as if she had aged fifty years when I spoke to her the following morning. I gave her all the positive information about Jack, but I don't know how much she actually heard. She was still very distressed and I told her not to worry and take as much time as she needed.

"They haven't released her body yet," she said to me quite distractedly. "The police, I mean, even though they have held the inquest. It was suicide whilst the mind—" She couldn't finish the sentence before sobbing. Charles took her in his arms and tried to calm her and I thought it best to leave them.

After lunch I collected the things that Jack would need and drove myself to the clinic, I didn't feel as if I could ask Charles for anything at the moment as he seemed to have enough on his plate.

Jack had settled in very well and I met his two personal trainers that were going to help with his recovery. He still couldn't speak well enough to make hisself understandable but he had some aids which helped to make him get understood and he was able to write but got frustrated with the time it took.

Jack was determined he was going to get better and when I left, I agreed to visit every other day as he didn't want me interrupting his regime which had been arranged for his recovery. Even after six weeks he had improved enough to come home, he was doing really well and when discussing him being at home with his own gym and swimming pool, it was felt it would be an even better arrangement.

One of his personal trainers and a nurse would be full time employed and live in. We both realised how lucky we were to afford this and in the end we donated enough money to have an indoor pool at the hospital because Jack would not have recovered so well without the help that he had received. The money was donated from the 'Chrissy Foundation' and gratefully received.

It felt so good to have Jack home, although he was far from completely recovered. He had come a long way. Jack got very frustrated and sometimes angry with the people closest to him, me included, but I did get some of my life back as it seemed I had been doing nothing but travelling backwards and forwards to clinics speaking to police and trying to keep our home functioning as normally as possible.

It took another twelve months before I can honestly say that Jack was anything like back to normal and even then when he was tired, his speech slurred and he would walk with a slight limp on his left side. But he did return to writing and recording he even did one or two-stage shows, but these exhausted him much too, much so they were vetoed.

I can't say that life went back to the way it was before because it didn't. Life seemed to be more sombre somehow. Julie never quite recovered and retired to a small Cotswold village and Charles only worked part time as security consultant. Eddie stayed with us for twelve months and then returned to Australia. I did miss him but he eventually wanted to be home and he took Susie's ashes to spread on an area she loved and where for a time she had been happy.

I'm still unable to walk into the studio. I still see that picture I had first seen when I had walked in that morning and I don't think it will ever leave my mind.

Jack's fans still stalk him. They camp outside the gates and write graffiti on the walls surrounding the property. 'We love you, Jack' they write and leave their names and undying devotion. We have it all cleaned off every so often but it soon reappears. Sometimes one or two of them get in to the grounds and have to be physically removed by the security people that we now employ by the dozen.

A strange thought crossed my mind the other day; I thought that if Jack had died that day, they still would not have left me alone. They would have claimed his ghost from me, believing that he belongs to them and not me. But he is mine, it's me he loves and holds and kisses each and every day and night and I love him too for always no matter how much anyone else believes that he is theirs, we will be together always and forever.